Praise for
HOME READING SERVICE

"In the tradition of the wittiest and wisest Mexican storytellers such as Jorge Ibargüengoitia, Juan Villoro, and Juan Pablo Villalobos, Fabio Morábito has written a fable about contemporary Mexico that is both hilariously entertaining and soberingly profound. *Home Reading Service* reads both as a beguiling page-turner and a tender and compassionate elegy about the social unraveling of a country devastated by corruption, organized crime, and collective solitude. Weeks after finishing this slim but muscular novel, I'm still haunted by it."

—Antonio Ruiz-Camacho, author of *Barefoot Dogs*

"I have always considered Morábito's work my main school of writing. Here, his precise, understated but always satisfying prose is preserved in Bauer's translation. *Home Reading Service* has contemporary violence as mere backdrop, and instead gives center stage to the suddenly rarefied acts of reading, of sharing, of paying—or not paying—attention. We are led through a series of quirky households and get to meet the unique underdogs who call them home. A humorous novel that entertains without ever giving up on poetry. A book with soul, despite all the swimming pools."

—Laia Jufresa, author of *Umami*

Home Reading Service

HOME READING SERVICE

Fabio Morábito

*Translated from the Spanish
by Curtis Bauer*

OTHER PRESS
NEW YORK

Originally published in Spanish as *El lector a domicilio*
in 2018 by Sexto Piso, Mexico City
Copyright © 2018 Fabio Morábito
Translation rights arranged by
Agencia Literaria CBQ SL
www.agencialiterariacbq.com
Translation copyright © 2021 Curtis Bauer

The two poems by Isabel Fraire that appear in this novel and are
reproduced in full in Spanish on pages 221–23 are reprinted
with the permission of the estate of Isabel Fraire.
Extracts from "Un signore maturo con un orecchio acerbo"
[A mature gentleman with an unripe ear] on pages 128–30 by Gianni Rodari.

Production editor: Yvonne E. Cárdenas
Text designer: Jennifer Daddio / Bookmark Design & Media Inc.
This book was set in Fairfield LH by
Alpha Design & Composition of Pittsfield, NH.

1 3 5 7 9 10 8 6 4 2

Library of Congress Cataloging-in-Publication Data
Names: Morábito, Fabio, 1955- author. | Bauer, Curtis, 1970- translator.
Title: Home reading service Fabio Morábito ; translated from the Spanish
by Curtis Bauer.
Other titles: Lector a domicilio. English
Description: New York : Other Press, [2021] | Originally published in Spanish
as El lector a domicilio in 2018 by Sexto Piso, Mexico City.
Identifiers: LCCN 2021005594 (print) | LCCN 2021005595 (ebook) |
ISBN 9781635420722 (paperback) | ISBN 9781635420739 (ebook)
Classification: LCC PQ7298.23.O724 L4313 2021 (print) |
LCC PQ7298.23.O724 (ebook) | DDC 863/.64—dc23
LC record available at https://lccn.loc.gov/2021005594
LC ebook record available at https://lccn.loc.gov/2021005595

Publisher's Note
This is a work of fiction. Names, characters, places, and incidents either
are the product of the author's imagination or are used fictitiously,
and any resemblance to actual persons, living or dead,
events, or locales is entirely coincidental.

PART ONE

I NEVER KNEW if the Jiménez brothers
had been married before. The thing is that
now, as old men, they lived together like
bachelors. Their house was a single-story
home, and judging by the long hallway that
connected the living room to the rest of the
house, it must have had a lot of rooms, or at
least I imagined it that way.

Luis, the one who looked a little dim-
witted, was crippled and seemed to be the
older of the two. It was difficult to know if
he really was a dimwit or not. While I read
out loud, he sat stiffly in his wheelchair,
without speaking or looking at me. As
for the sensible-looking brother, Carlos,

everything about him annoyed me: his smarmy gestures and that sarcastic little smile sewn across his mouth. The servant, an indigenous woman, always opened the door for me, and then she'd disappear down the long hallway and wouldn't show her face again; I was never offered a cup of coffee or a glass of water in that house, ever. The two brothers would arrive immediately, Carlos pushing Luis in his wheelchair, and they'd position themselves about ten feet away from me, an absurd arrangement that made it necessary for me to raise my voice while I read to them. When I asked them, on my first visit, if they could move a little closer, Carlos told me that Luis couldn't stand the proximity of other people and that such a distance was necessary to keep him from getting nervous. The dimwit ignored me, like I said, looking out the window the whole time or at his brother, who never took his eyes off me, and I tried to look at the two of them as little as possible.

When I finished reading, I took out the paperwork they needed to sign to document my visit. It confirmed that I was completing a specified number of community-service hours. It was the only time Luis came out of his trancelike state because, as some sort of concession, Carlos allowed him to sign the form; Luis looked proud as his trembling hand traced his crude scribble, meanwhile Carlos studied me as if he wanted to know what crime I'd committed.

They'd chosen Dostoyevsky's *Crime and Punishment* for me to read, and it was in the middle of our third session when Luis unexpectedly opened his mouth to tell me, "I've realized that you're not paying any attention to what you're reading."

I raised my head suddenly, because it was the first time I'd heard his voice.

"What did you say?" I asked him. After three reading sessions, in which I hadn't heard him speak a single word, I would have sworn he was not only a dimwit but mute as well.

"You don't pay any attention to what you're reading," the old man repeated, not looking at me but at the window.

"Luis, stop that, will you?" his brother scolded, but Luis continued, without taking his eyes off the window, as if speaking to it and not to me. "You come to our house, you sit on our sofa, open your briefcase, and with that magnificent voice of yours you read without understanding anything, as if we weren't worthy of your attention."

"Please Luis, we've talked about this! Don't be difficult," Carlos told him.

"I'm not being difficult. You know I'm right," said Luis, who apparently was neither mute nor a dimwit. However, he didn't show the slightest sign of anger, and the incongruity between his face and what he said, coupled with the fact that he spoke while looking at the window, as if he didn't consider me worthy of his attention, made his reproach even more offensive.

"Let the young man continue reading, will you?"

"If you want to keep listening to him, go ahead," Luis replied, "but it's clear that we don't interest him in the slightest. Have you noticed that he's always looking at his watch?"

So Luis, who seemed to ignore me, was actually aware of every movement I made. I did in fact look at my watch all the time, because reading in that house was agonizing, starting with that absurd distance the brothers put between themselves and me, forcing me to strain my voice. The dimwit who wasn't a dimwit went on the offensive again: "Why don't you admit that I'm right?"

He asked without turning to look at me, as if instead of speaking to me, he was repeating the words someone was whispering in his ear. I had a hunch and looked at Carlos's mouth. While Luis spoke, Carlos's mouth moved almost imperceptibly. My heart beat faster. I realized that the one who'd been speaking the whole time wasn't Luis, who was indeed mute and a dimwit, but Carlos, his brother, who was a ventriloquist and whose lips trembled slightly when Luis opened his mouth. They must have spent hours rehearsing this so they could entertain themselves at the expense of their guests.

I closed the book, opened my briefcase, and put the book inside.

"What are you doing? Aren't you going to continue reading?" Carlos asked me.

I looked at both of them, at Carlos sitting in his worn-out armchair and at Luis in his wheelchair, one beside the other. Now I understood our ten-foot separation. They needed it for their ruse to work. As I removed the visitation form they needed to sign from my briefcase, I said to Carlos, "You're right, when I come here I don't understand a thing I read to you. You could have told me directly. Or do you always use your brother like a puppet to tell your visitors what you think of them?"

I stood up and he recoiled slightly, afraid perhaps that I'd hit him. He must have remembered that I was working off my probation by doing these home readings, and he was afraid of me. But I'd stood up only so his dimwit brother could sign the form and I could leave.

"You still have twenty minutes left," he told me.

"Sign it," I told Luis, shoving the paperwork under his nose. The two brothers looked at each other, then Luis scribbled his dull signature and I ripped the form out of his hands.

"I'll file a complaint with your superiors," Carlos snapped, as I was placing the form in my briefcase.

"File your complaint. I'll tell them that you treat your brother like a circus puppet, and the people on the city council won't be very happy about that."

I turned and walked toward the door. When I opened it, Carlos said, "We know what you did."

I turned my head and looked at both of them.

"We know everything," Luis added with his puppet voice, not looking at me, but out the window.

IT WAS THANKS to Father Clark, my sister Ofelia's confessor, that I was given the home reader job. He was the head of a Christian association that helped senior citizens; it was funded through private donations and was affiliated with the local government. Since he knew the mayor personally, he pulled a few strings and, instead of cleaning bathrooms in some hospital or prison, I was assigned the job of reading books to the elderly and infirm, visiting them in their homes. My university experience worked to my advantage, and my "beautiful manly voice," as Father Clark called it, was ideal for this line of work.

He was a tall, heavyset man and gave the impression of having chosen the wrong vocation. It was hard to imagine him crammed inside a confessional, listening to the sins of the devout who attended mass on Sundays. His forceful voice, with a thick American accent, didn't seem to be the most suitable for conveying soft words of admonishment or consolation. Ofelia held him in high esteem, and I suspected that she was also in love with him. In the interview we had in his office, he made a few recommendations, the main one was that I shouldn't accept anything to eat or drink in the houses I visited as a home reader, except a glass of water or cup of coffee.

I was assigned seven houses; most of the people were older and retired. I was on familiar ground with the elderly because I lived with my father, who had bone and prostate cancer. My mother had died seven years before and Papá never fully recovered. His cancer did the rest. Celeste, his caregiver, lived with us and was essentially the only person who could communicate with him. I tried to have breakfast with him and give him updates about family and friends, though I made most of it up. Between his hearing loss and the onset of senile dementia, it was hard to know how much of what I told him he actually understood. He used a walker to get around and spent his days sleeping in bed or in front of the television. Ofelia took care of the house expenses, was the one who bought his medication and took Celeste to the supermarket. I was in charge of the furniture store. In charge is one way of putting it, because the one who did all the work was Jaime, our one employee, and I went over the accounts and orders with him.

Every now and then we took Papá out for a drive. My driver's license was suspended indefinitely after the accident, so Ofelia would drive on such excursions. Those were the few times that the two of us talked, while my father sat in the front passenger seat. We'd take the old highway to Tres Marías, where there were several open-air restaurants that sold quesadillas. We ate in the

car, because for some reason Papá seemed to hear better
in there and we could have a more fluid conversation.
Those moments of coexistence were the best our family
ever shared. In the middle of that pine landscape, the
fog coming down from the hills, and the black smoke
smelling like burned oak rising from the kitchens,
Ofelia and I left our squabbles aside and Papá enjoyed
his squash blossom and huitlacoche quesadillas. One
day, however, he had to take a shit and we needed to
get him out of the car and find a secluded place among
the trees. Holding on to me and Ofelia, he squatted and
pushed in vain and ended up insulting us, accusing us of
not knowing how to help him. He was right, neither of
us were any good at that kind of thing. He slammed into
the wall of our inexperience; it was as if we belonged
to some other species altogether. We never needed
Celeste more than we did then; she knew what words
and tone to use with him to get his bowels working. I
felt useless and, in that moment, hated Ofelia; it was
unfair, but I expected her to have some skill I didn't, as
if by being a woman, she should possess the particular
talents our caregiver had. We ended up fighting right
there instead of helping my father out of his fix, and
it was then that he, finding himself entrusted to such
clumsy hands, decided to take matters into his own,
intensified his concentration, and let go what he had to
let go, as if he were reproaching us for the totality of our
immaturity and selfishness. It was, in a way, a lesson in

dignity, extracted from the most undignified part of his body, and it was also his farewell as our father, because after that excursion he seemed to have given up on us. Like an iceberg emerging from the frozen continent to emigrate to its dilution, he began to treat us from then on with a subtle, almost smiling indifference and only had eyes for Celeste.

Before we hired a caregiver, Ofelia and I had thought of putting him in an old-age home, nursing homes as they are now called euphemistically. Cuernavaca, better known as the City of Eternal Spring, abounds with them, and over the course of a few weeks my father and I visited half a dozen. The idea was that Papá would be there during the day and return to the house to sleep, so he could meet people and not spend the whole day watching TV. The promotional pamphlets for these homes usually show a couple of smiling old people on the cover, almost always with European or North American features, and the pictures of the interior suggest a sense of comfort and elegance. Old age is presented as a permanent vacation, full of social and recreational activities, and there are impeccable lawns, the indispensable pool, rooms with fireplaces, and smiling nurses. But when you entered one of these establishments, there was a different reality. The impeccable lawns weren't missing, nor the pool nor the rooms with fireplaces, but what seemed like a cheerful hotel, was in fact a hospital in disguise. The smell

of ammonia on the floors gave it away, the perfectly
geometrical placement of the sofas and armchairs,
as well as that air of isolation wheezing through the
corridors. The old-timers didn't meet amicably like
the photos attempted to make us believe but milled
about by themselves, most of them didn't even leave
their rooms. The recreational activities consisted of an
invited clown or singer once or twice a week, and there
were also the ever-present craft workshops for painting,
ceramics, and papier-mâché. The script was repeated
almost identically in all the homes we visited. It's not for
you, I'd tell Papá as we were leaving, and he'd ask if it
was because of the price. No, the price is fine, but it's a
mortuary, I'd respond, and he'd be quiet and dissatisfied,
as if he thought that the shimmering blue pool and the
green lawn were all he needed to feel at home. After the
fifth or sixth visit, I decided that Papá would die in our
house, far from the smell of ammonia and rooms with
fireplaces. It was the best I could do for him and that
same afternoon I started looking for a full-time caregiver.

WHEN CARLOS JIMÉNEZ TALKED with Father
Clark to accuse me of ending my session twenty minutes
early and having forced them to sign the visitation form
against their will, the priest asked me to meet him in
his office, where he scrutinized me with those eyes
that were as celestial as they were expressionless. I told

him that I had indeed left the Jiménez brothers' house twenty minutes before concluding the reading session, requesting that they sign my exit form, but it was a lie that I'd forced them to do so.

"And do you mind telling me why you ended your reading twenty minutes early?"

I told him that the lucid brother had criticized the way I read, not by facing me head-on but by using his mute brother, who's a total dimwit. Father Clark didn't understand what I was talking about and I had to explain what happened in detail.

"Señor Carlos is a ventriloquist and he spoke to me as if it were his brother who was speaking. The brother, the dimwit, moves his lips like a fish, while Señor Carlos speaks through him. The mute doesn't understand a thing, because if you speak to him, he doesn't even look at you."

The priest stood up suddenly, pushing his chair back and hitting the wall where there was already a mark in the plaster, an indication that this was his usual way of getting out of his chair, and he walked to the window with his hands clasped behind his back.

"Eduardo," he said in his gringo accent, "you should have reported everything you are telling me when it happened. Now you find yourself at a disadvantage, because there is a complaint against you, you are accused of aggressive behavior. I am going to have to take matters into my own hands."

He looked outside. He was clearly excited, and I thought that behind his bland appearance he hid a belligerent side. It must have been this that made him so attractive in Ofelia's eyes. However, as organized as she was, I had my doubts that she'd tolerate her house filling up with marks on her walls, like those the priest left when he got up from his swivel chair.

"I am going to talk to the Jiménez brothers, to see if I can convince them to withdraw their complaint," he told me. "You were lucky they spoke with me and not with the people on the city council. A formal complaint would not look very good for you right now, Eduardo."

He put out his hand to signal that the meeting had ended, and he told me that he'd keep me informed. I thanked him and left his office. I ran into Ofelia at the entrance to the building. I asked what she was doing there, and she told me she'd come to see Father Clark. If you wait for me, I'll drive you home, she told me, and I asked for her car keys so I could wait for her in the parking lot. Inside the car, seeing that she was taking a while, I started it up. I hadn't started a car engine since my driver's license had been taken away four months earlier. The place was empty, so I put it in first gear and let out the clutch. I drove one lap around the parking lot in second, then another one, and continued making laps in second gear. I thought that my own life seemed to be stuck in second gear; I hardly saw anyone and spent my mornings in the Sanborns de Piedra restaurant chatting with Gladis and the other waitresses. My few friends had distanced themselves from me or I'd distanced myself from them, which one wasn't clear yet. In a way, I took pleasure in that distance and was trying to extend it, because I hoped to transform myself in some way that would surprise them when we saw each other again. However, since I hadn't received the slightest indication from them that they wanted to reconnect, I started to believe that their separation was real, not contrived like mine, and that I was really going to end up alone, going in circles, the way Ofelia found me when she finally appeared in the parking lot. I stopped and got into the passenger seat so she could take the wheel. Since she didn't ask me anything about my interview with Father Clark, I suspected that he'd told her everything already, which annoyed me.

"Why didn't you ask me what we talked about instead of asking the priest?" I said.

"I didn't ask him anything," she snapped.

"I bet he told you about the Jiménez brothers."

"He only told me that they were canceling your readings."

"And did he tell you why?"

"No, I was going to ask you that."

I didn't know if I should believe her, so I kept quiet.

"Aren't you going to tell me?" she asked.

Instead of answering I asked, "How can you like him?"

"Who?"

"Father Clark."

She blushed. "Who told you I like him?"

Her eyes were shooting fire and for an instant I saw the Ofelia of my childhood, when we got along so well.

"It's obvious, because of how you talk about him."

"That's the stupidest thing I've ever heard!"

We didn't speak to each other the rest of the drive home. She stayed for dinner because she had to look over a few bills with Celeste and, while we ate, I recounted what had happened at the Jiménez brothers' house. I did it hoping I might amuse my father with an interesting story, but even though he watched me the whole time, his expression remained absent and I doubt he followed a single word I said. Celeste was the most impressed; she didn't know that such a thing as a ventriloquist existed. Ofelia and I explained that these people are capable of speaking with their stomachs and we gave her a little demonstration, me taking the role of the ventriloquist and Ofelia the puppet that opens its mouth, but our little show was so bad that Celeste ended up more confused than before. Papá didn't laugh even once, and when we finished, he nodded to Celeste that he wanted to go to bed.

Once the cancer set into his legs, he suffered from bouts of severe pain that was even more acute when he made certain movements, like getting into bed, and on this occasion Ofelia and I heard him moan in agony. The

TV was on, so we concentrated on the screen, waiting for Papá to stop moaning.

"This is no way to live," I told her.

"We can't do anything about it."

"There has to be some way to end this."

"Sometimes you scare me when I hear you talk," she said.

"You come two or three times a week, you stay for a while and then you leave; I'm always here, I hear him when he whimpers because of his bones or when he can't shit, and then he starts to insult Celeste. Every day it's the same. After all that moaning, he stops being your father and turns into something else."

"So, you'd be able to do it," she said.

"He'd thank me for it, but I don't have the nerve."

We sat in silence, not taking our eyes off the TV. Then I reminded her about the cat.

"What cat?"

"The one they set on fire," I told her.

We were kids and I'd found the cat in a vacant lot close to our house, beneath some rocks, hairless and in agony, its skin dark and translucent from the burn, its pure white teeth in stark contrast to its partially charred body. It hardly moved, though, incredibly, it was still alive after the torture it had received, most likely at the hands of some hooligan kids in the neighborhood. They'd thrown gasoline on it, because the place reeked of it, and

I thought they must have been the ones who'd hidden it under the rocks, because the sight of the animal writhing in its last spasms of life must have scared the hell out of them. Don't look, Ofelia had ordered, and I moved back a few steps, obeying her, the way one obeys a goddess. She picked up the biggest rock she could find, lifted it with both hands, and I heard the crinkle of its skull when it broke; then she put the rock back in its place, sealing that rudimentary grave, and for the next several days I'd walk by the lot and stop for a few seconds, long enough to make sure that the little mound of rocks was still there.

"How can you compare that with this? Sometimes I think you've lost it," she said without looking at me.

I didn't say anything, knowing that the memory still tormented her just like it did me, and because of that neither of us could ever have a cat.

After she separated from Rodolfo, her husband, she'd had an attack of Catholic fervor that led her to join a Bible circle, and since then she carried a Bible with her everywhere she went, and she'd open it at the slightest excuse to read one or two verses. Since you're so hooked on that book, you should let me read it when you're done with it, I'd say, mocking her. She started to read passages to Celeste, who listened attentively to her explications. If there's one thing I can't stand it's when someone lectures another with the book open in her hand, while the other listens with her head bowed, and seeing Ofelia given over

to that labor of proselytizing made me sick to my stomach.
Where had that intrepid Ofelia gone, the one who'd meant
the world to me, who was more important to me than my
father and mother? Don't look, she'd told me that morning
in the abandoned lot, moving me away so I wouldn't see
the animal as it continued breathing, and part of me
still adored her for doing that. Since her marriage we'd
become strangers, and her divorce, instead of bringing us
back together, had pushed us further apart. Bible circles
infested our city as much as, if not more than, swimming
pools, which we had more of than any other city in the
world, as we'd been told with a certain sense of pride
since we were children, as if it were some honorary title.
Bibles and swimming pools were the two bastions of our
desolately uncultured community.

SINCE PAPÁ WOULD soon be unable to sign any
official documents, Ofelia and I decided to put his bank
account in my name. I went to the Banorte branch office
early one day and Rosario, the director, greeted me with
a hug and asked about my father. She knew him well,
so I told her the truth: "He's depressed, distant, and he's
losing his hearing."

She shook her head and told me that one of these
days she'd come by to say hello.

"He always asks me about you," I lied. Papá didn't ask
about anyone these days, but I knew a visit from Rosario

would lift his spirits, because he was always a little smitten with this short, constantly moving, middle-aged woman who painstakingly managed his scarce savings. He liked short women who were quick to laugh.

Rosario took me to the cubicle of Señorita Consuelo Mijares, who was going to take care of my paperwork, and that's where I spent more than an hour signing forms. When I finished, I went by Rosario's cubicle to say goodbye and take her picture, because I knew Papá would love to have a picture of her, but she wasn't there, and Mario, the manager in the cubicle beside hers, told me she'd left the office.

I left the bank and went to the furniture store, where Jaime showed me the merchandise that had come in from Querétaro: three mahogany desks and three build-in wardrobes ready for installation. It was time to take the delivery truck in for its annual inspection, so I gave him a five-hundred-peso bill. Before they took away my driver's license, I was the one who handled the truck inspection.

"Did Güero come by?" I asked him.

"No."

I hadn't intended to ask him about Güero, but I couldn't help myself. Güero stopped in to collect his protection fee (that's what he called it) at the beginning of every month, more punctual than Benito Juárez's birthday, and I tried to show my only employee that such a thing didn't keep me up at night. Jaime had been working in the furniture store for six years, he'd become indispensable and the thought of him quitting made me sick to my stomach.

We'd hidden the envelope with the money for Güero in one of the crossbars of the Swiss bunk beds so it wouldn't come into contact with the money in the cash register. There was no other reason for this separation than it being dirty money, not because we'd earned it that way but because it was going to wind up in dirty hands, and I preferred to keep it away from the clean money, the money that allowed Jaime and my family to make a living.

That afternoon I had two home readings: *The Mysterious Island* by Jules Verne, with the Vigil family, and Dino Buzzati's *The Tartar Steppe*, with Colonel Atarriaga, who'd fall asleep like clockwork after I read three pages.

The Vigils were a family of tailors. They were devout in how they arranged themselves on the sofa: The father, the mother, the grandmother, and the three little boys always sat in the same order, and they always observed absolute silence. On my first visit the mother opened the door for me, the rest of the family was already seated, and mounded on the dining-room table were several pieces of fabric and three sewing machines. They greeted me by nodding their heads, and when I finished reading, the mother thanked me and walked me to the door. The following afternoon the electricity went off

while I was reading. Although it was beginning to get
dark outside, there was still enough light coming through
the window, so I continued. Yet I noticed that they
weren't really listening to what I was reading. I asked
what was wrong. The mother raised a finger to her lips
and told me that they needed to see my lips in order to
understand what I was reading. That's how I realized the
whole family was deaf. I told Ofelia what had happened,
who then told Father Clark, who then spoke to the city
council to look into whether the family of tailors was
ideal for the home reading program. He found out that
the grandmother was the only one born deaf, while the
father and mother weren't mute because they'd become
deaf when they were children and already knew how
to speak, and the same had happened with their three
boys. In short, all of them could read lips, including
the grandmother, so they could understand what I read
perfectly, providing that I clearly articulated each word.
And that's what I started to do, emphasizing each word,
each sentence, which meant I was exhausted by the time
I finished those sessions.

When I arrived at the Vigil house the mother opened
the door, as usual. The grandmother and boys made
their gesticulations of hello, and I noticed the father
was missing. His wife told me he was sick, but I didn't
know if I should believe her because the week before
I'd had a disagreement with him, and I thought it was
an excuse not to see me. It happened like this. Because

of the effort required to read in that house, after half
an hour I requested a five-minute break and asked for a
glass of water. The eldest boy went to get it, and shortly
after, we heard something crash on the floor. I said we
heard, because the two kids and I turned toward the
kitchen. The parents and grandmother were unfazed,
but they could see from our reaction that something
had happened, and the mother got up and went to the
kitchen, followed by the grandmother. I stayed with
Señor Vigil and the two little ones.

"So they do hear," I said, pointing to his children.

He didn't say anything. The boys had lowered their
eyes and didn't dare look at their father, as if they'd done
something terribly wrong showing me that they could
hear. This made me angry because I was torturing my
throat for this family and I thought I deserved an answer,
so I insisted: "Your children can hear, can't they?"

"They can hear, but they're deaf."

"If they can hear, they're not deaf," I countered as
politely as I could.

"You wouldn't understand."

I decided not to argue, we resumed the reading, and
later, on my way home, it occurred to me that the three
boys, as children of deaf parents, had adjusted their lives
around the deafness of their parents and grandmother.
They knew how to read lips and they were fluent in sign
language; therefore, they lived like deaf people, perhaps
even communicating with each other that way, even

though they could hear and, most likely, they could also speak. But had they ever spoken? Or had they grown accustomed to their mother speaking for them, hardly opening their mouths like their father and preferring to speak in sign language, like deaf people? They were fake-deaf, and I wondered if they were aware of this.

The mother was smiling when she opened the door, something peculiar for her, and I noticed that Señor Vigil's absence contributed to a more relaxed interaction among the family. While I read they laughed on a few occasions, something that had never happened before, and I couldn't resist the temptation to ask if they liked the Verne novel or if we wanted to read a different book. The mother said that once you start a book you have to finish it.

"Yes, but if it's boring, you should read something else," I said.

The grandmother, who was the only mute and had never said two words to me, so the expression goes, made me understand, through her gestures, the same thing as the mother, that is, that one should never stop reading a book halfway through, and I suspected that this dogma came down from the father, and it occurred to me that if the prejudices of parents in the average household are difficult to eradicate, in a deaf family's home it's even more so because it's a home much less exposed to outside opinions. I asked them, then, what school the kids went to.

"They don't go to school," the mother said.

"But who teaches them to read and write?"

"They don't know how."

I closed the book, astonished. "And what are you waiting for?"

"None of us can read and write. We're deaf."

"There are schools for the deaf," I said enthusiastically.

The grandmother got up and left the living room. I imagined that she was going to talk with her son, the father of the boys, and that he'd come out in a minute and ask me to leave. I could see myself summoned by Father Clark again, another complaint against me. But the boys' father didn't appear, and the mother, faced with my prolonged silence, asked me if I was going to continue reading. I wanted to tell her that they couldn't deny their children the opportunity to go to school, much less force them to be deaf when they weren't, but instead I opened the book again and continued reading. I was so upset that I lowered my head unintentionally, blocking their view of my lips. I noticed that they were looking at each other and I asked them what was wrong.

"Your lips, please," the mother said.

I apologized and asked them to tell me at what point they'd stopped seeing my lips.

"Where Axel's hat falls off," they answered.

I started looking for the episode they mentioned on the previous page.

"It's further back," the mother said.

I went back another page and looked for the word hat. I didn't have the slightest idea where it could be. I not only didn't remember Axel had lost his hat but I also didn't remember who Axel was.

"Are you sure that was the sentence?" I asked only to buy a little time while my finger swept over each line unsuccessfully and a revealing blush colored my face.

The mother didn't answer me. They'd just discovered my secret: I didn't pay attention to what I read. At that moment the grandmother returned to her place on the sofa. Finally, the blessed word appeared beneath my finger.

"Here it is!" I exclaimed, and the three boys gave a shout of glee that, in spite of myself, made me smile. The mother and grandmother laughed as well. I'd just shown them that I was deafer than they were, since I couldn't hear myself, and that embarrassed me. Luckily, something unexpected occurred that shook the family, mobilizing all of them as if they were a single body. The mother got up and went to her sick husband's room, followed swiftly by the grandmother, and one of the boys, the middle one, went to the kitchen; the youngest hesitated, followed his brother, and I was left alone with the eldest, the only one who hadn't stood up. He smiled at me and I smiled at him. Then it occurred to me to stand up and approach the sofa to look at the painting hanging above it. While I pretended to look at it, I pulled a coin out of my pocket and let it fall behind me. The sound of the coin hitting the floor made him look down, and he bent over to pick it up.

"See?" I said to him. "You heard the coin fall. Look," and I dropped it again. "Did you hear that?"

He nodded yes.

"You're not deaf, and your brothers aren't deaf. Keep the coin, play the same game with them and you'll see that I'm right."

The boy ran to the kitchen with the coin, a minute later the mother came into the living room to tell me we couldn't continue the reading because her husband had fallen out of bed, hurting his shoulder, and they were going to call a doctor. How had they heard the father fall, if they were deaf?

"I didn't hear anything," I said.

She pointed to the floor and walls and told me she'd perceived the vibrations produced by the impact of his fall. She explained it with such naturalness that she convinced me. It must be a specific faculty of the deaf, one those of us who can hear and speak have lost. I put the Verne book in my briefcase and she walked me to the door. Already with one foot outside, I told her, "I could teach your kids how to read and write, if you want. I wouldn't charge you anything, it would be part of my community service."

I didn't know if they'd allow me to use it for my community service, but I felt like I owed them

something after the embarrassing performance I'd given
a few minutes earlier. She looked at me, frightened,
as if she'd always feared that moment when someone
would offer to educate her children, and I suspected that
they'd walled themselves up in their illiterate deaf world,
reluctant to open themselves to the outside, except for
the connection they had with their clients, and that I
was their only real link to the world.

"Think about my offer, you have intelligent children,"
I said, and she looked at me with hostility, as if the word
intelligent made her uncomfortable. Maybe she didn't
want her children to be intelligent but only wanted them
to be good tailors. It was hard not to see her point, after
I'd demonstrated how precarious my intelligence was,
that it didn't save me from straying from what I read,
and the depth of my deafness, which didn't allow me to
notice any vibrations through the walls or floor.

That night I told Celeste about my discovery in the
Vigil house, and I was surprised that she agreed with the
parents' decision to keep their boys out of school. She
told me that, because they were deaf, their classmates
would have made fun of them. I told her that they really
weren't deaf, that they acted like they were deaf because
they lived in a house with deaf people and besides, there
were schools for the deaf, where they would have been
taught to read and write. In the passion of my tirade I'd
forgotten that Celeste herself was illiterate, and she fell
silent after that. I'd hurt her feelings, made her feel like

I was reprimanding her for this flaw, and I tried to make things right. "I'm not saying this about you. You've made something of your life, you know how to take care of yourself, but these boys, what kind of life will they have without some kind of education?"

I was afraid she'd answer: And this is a good life, Eduardo, caring for an old man who hardly speaks, seven days a week, never seeing my only child, who lives far away, and that's not to mention you, Eduardo, even quieter than your father, even though you're young and you live in this house as if it were a hotel, and you never smile or joke around?

She said none of this but kept quiet, and I thought that, if she could choose, she wouldn't have thought twice about changing my father's house for the deaf one, even if it meant becoming deaf herself. She'd have more opportunities to talk there than in our house. The phone rang. It was Father Clark. I have taken matters into my own hands, he told me after we greeted each other. He liked that phrase, apparently. Some foreigners tend to fall in love with certain structures in our language and they use them for everything. I met a German woman who used to say, "It remains to be seen," and repeated it whenever she could. "It remains to be seen if it will rain later," she'd say seeing the sky covered with clouds, or "It remains to be seen how badly my daughter-in-law dresses." Father Clark liked to take matters into his own hands and used the expression "That seems reasonable to me." He told me that he'd spoken with Carlos Jiménez on the phone, and he was willing to withdraw his complaint against me, provided that I completed the twenty minutes of reading I'd taken from them.

"I don't trust those people," I told him. "I'll go if you come with me. I want a witness who can testify that I fulfilled the remaining twenty minutes of reading that I'm short."

"That seems reasonable to me," the priest said, "but I cannot go with you, Eduardo. I am very busy. Ask Celeste to go with you."

That he knew about Celeste confirmed that he and my sister were really close. We hung up, and I asked Celeste if she wanted to come with me to the house of the gentlemen who spoke with their stomach the following Thursday. She asked me if she had to dress up and I said no.

"Then I'll go," she said.

A CAR ACCIDENT three or four years ago had left Margó Benítez wheelchair-bound. She was the one who told me, before the Jiménez brothers, that I didn't pay attention to what I was reading.

"You don't seem to care about what you read," she blurted out when I walked into her house, still standing, holding the briefcase where I kept the book we were reading, *The Turn of the Screw* by Henry James. I thought she revealed a certain lack of refinement on her part saying it that way without first asking me to sit down. Aurelia, the maid, an ugly woman with a prominent bust, came in with the coffeepot and the aroma of the coffee engulfed the living room. As she bent over to fill our cups, she let me see the great size of her boobs and, seeing that I was still standing, she asked why I wasn't sitting down, to which Margó Benítez, realizing her lack of manners, exclaimed, "Forgive me, Eduardo! I've kept you standing there, holding your briefcase and waiting. Please sit."

Aurelia went back to the kitchen and I sat down, took a sip of coffee, and said, "If I read out loud, I don't understand what I'm reading."

"No, you are in love with your own voice," Margó Benítez replied. "You have a seductive voice and you let it do all the work for you." She was silent for a moment, then she added, "Let's try a different book. Maybe, if it's a book I'm familiar with, your reading style won't bother me so much. Do you know Daphne du Maurier? She's an English writer."

I told her I didn't, she called Aurelia and asked her to go to her room and bring the book that was on her desk. Aurelia's daughter, an eight-year-old girl, ugly like her mother, followed her, giving me a frightened look as they passed. Aurelia came back with the book and Margó indicated that she should give it to me. Mother and daughter went back to the kitchen, and I opened the book to the first page and cleared my voice, ready to start reading.

"You are upset," Margó said.

"Why?"

"You haven't even looked at the title of the book."

It was true, I hadn't looked. I closed the book to read the title: *My Cousin Rachel.*

"I have a problem with titles," I told her. "I usually skip them. I notice that they're there, but I don't read them."

"For goodness' sake, I've never met anyone like you, Eduardo. When you read out loud you don't understand what you are reading, and when you see a title you skip it."

She straightened the hem of her skirt. Although it's difficult to know the height of someone you've only seen in a wheelchair, she was, without a doubt, tall. I asked her why she'd signed up for the home reading program, since she was a cultured person used to reading on her own.

"Eduardo, it's clear that you are still in your youth. Because I get bored and no one visits me, it's that simple. And you have a beautiful manly voice, though you don't understand anything you read."

"I try to read as best as I can."

"You have already told me that." She laughed. "Don't pay any attention to me, I've become a bitter woman since this happened to me," she pointed to the wheelchair, "and I see flaws everywhere."

I was going to ask her what had happened, but I decided to keep quiet. It was none of my business. Besides, it's not easy to ask an attractive older woman how she came to be shackled to a wheelchair for the rest of her life.

She asked me to read. I opened the book to the first page, but I closed it again to read the title: *My Cousin Rachel*. It was a good title, suggesting an unhappy love story, like love between cousins usually is. I maintained my focus throughout the first page, but on the second the words began to march around, becoming meaningless before my eyes. I stopped to look at my host, who asked me what was wrong.

"I got lost."

"I know, I can tell almost immediately when your voice and head go in different directions," and she told me she was fond of the opera, that she took lessons from a voice coach and that had made her sensitive to voice modulations. I wondered how she could sing opera with that slightly rusty voice of hers, and had I been a little more daring, I would have asked her to sing something.

"There are many singers who do the same thing as you, Eduardo, they sing without knowing what they're singing," she said. "Pure voice and lung."

I asked where she had performed, and she replied that she'd never sung in public. She lacked the courage and regretted that.

"I could have been an admirable mezzo-soprano; not an eminence but, yes, admirable. And then this happened," she said, pointing again to her wheelchair. "And it's hard to sing sitting down."

THE NEXT DAY I found this poem by the Mexican poet Isabel Fraire, which my father had copied out by hand in one of his old account books when he still kept track of the furniture store sales and expenses:

> Your skin, like sheets of sand, and sheets of water
>   swirling
> your skin, with its louring mandolin brilliance
> your skin, where my skin arrives as if coming home
> and lights a silenced lamp
> your skin, that nourishes my eyes
> and wears my name like a new dress
> your skin a mirror where my skin recognizes me
> and my lost hand comes back from my childhood and
>   reaches
> this present moment and greets me
> your skin, where at last
> I am with myself

Isabel Fraire was his favorite poet, and he always said that she was by far the best poet in Mexico. Sometimes he'd read a poem to me and Ofelia, one of hers or someone else's, and when he finished both of us would be quiet, because we thought that was how you had to respond to a poem, as if it were a prayer, without offering any opinion about it. We thought all poems, by the mere fact of being poems, were good and that judging them was foolish. But one day my father read us "Nocturne for Rosario" by Manuel Acuña, telling us that it was the worst Mexican poem of all time. Not only did I not think it was bad but I found it moving, and I hid that feeling as best as I could, because my father paused every two or three lines to make fun of it. That day I understood that there were good and bad poems, that it was possible after reading them to say "I like it" and "I don't like it," and that there were bad poems that could be liked a lot, like "Nocturne for Rosario," and good poems that can leave you indifferent. I wasn't very interested in poetry, but I was no longer afraid of it, and from then on, if I came across a poem in a magazine or newspaper, I'd read it to see if it was one of the good ones or the bad ones, one of those I liked or one of those that left me unmoved.

The poem was written in Papá's handwriting, so I thought it was his, and though I understood it from the first line to the last, I decided it was one of the bad ones. Discovering that my father, that rather melancholy man, a steady breadwinner for his family, wrote poems, didn't fill me with a lot of enthusiasm. There was something pitiful in imagining him gripped by some lyric rapture, erotic as well, because it was an erotic poem, and I was relieved when I turned the page over and read Isabel Fraire's name under the last line. I reread the poem and it instantly transformed before my eyes. Not only was it good, it was wonderful. In truth, it was the first wonderful poem I'd read, and the fact that Papá had written it out by hand confirmed for me that it was truly good. I decided to copy it myself and read it to Margó Benítez on my next visit because she was the only one of my hosts who could appreciate a contemporary erotic poem. I sat at the dining-room table while Celeste was in the kitchen and Papá slept in his room, and when I finished copying it, I read it out loud. I didn't like how it sounded and I remembered that Papá used to read us poems in the neutral tone one reads a business letter, because according to him you had to let the poem make itself clear without dressing it up with trembles and shivers. I reread it that way and noticed a sudden silence in the kitchen. I turned my head and saw Celeste standing in the doorway with one hand on her chest and her breathing agitated, and I asked her what was wrong.

"Nothing. I heard you speaking out loud and I thought you were calling me, Eduardo. That's why I came in."

"I was reading a poem by a Mexican poet; my father had written it out by hand," I told her. "I'm practicing so I can read it this afternoon."

"Great. Please, don't let me stop you," and she went back to the kitchen.

But now I didn't feel like continuing and I doubted whether I should read the poem to Margó Benítez. The mere thought of her blushing and pressing her hand to her chest like Celeste would have mortified me. I went to the kitchen for a glass of water, Celeste stood oddly motionless in front of the sink, her back turned to me, and I knew she was crying, so I walked out, went to my room, and realized that she'd heard that poem before, probably because my father had read it to her. That upset me more than if he'd written it himself, because it further exposed the depth of his solitude and his detachment from his children. Why had Celeste cried when she heard that poem? Were they tears of love? I grappled with the image of the two of them kissing and hugging each other, which I dismissed as something ridiculous, and the same discomfort I'd felt reading the poem, thinking it was my father's, struck me, an affair had quite possibly been going on in our house for the last several years, without me and my sister knowing about it. I was standing beside the window and I looked at the sink where Celeste scrubbed Papá's clothes when they were covered with urine and sometimes something worse, with that *squish-squash, squish-squash* that had become a permanent sound in the house. She'd been taking care of him for three years, cleaning him, getting him out of bed and putting him back, handling his most intimate parts, where I'm sure my mother had never gone, and I wondered if out of that other *squish-squash* something like infatuation couldn't emerge, all the coarseness and quiet, everything disguised as jokes and fits of rage one could want, but in the end falling in love, with poetry readings included.

I felt like an intruder in that house, my father's house, and I thought that maybe Papá would have been happier if I had left, because then he would have had the freedom to have a proper marriage with Celeste, with its quarrels, its embraces, its resentments, and its secrets.

I got dressed, put the sheet of paper where I'd copied Isabel Fraire's poem into my briefcase, and left.

I went to the furniture store, where I thought I'd wait around for a few minutes just to make an appearance, but Jaime showed me some outstanding accounts he wanted to go over and I had to give up eating lunch at Sanborns de Piedra as I'd planned. When we sat at the desk, he told me that Güero had come by that morning to pick up the envelope with the money. I nodded, avoiding his eyes, because I knew that Jaime thought every bit of this was disgraceful, most of all dealing with Güero, an ex-employee of the furniture store, not to mention the first employee my father had hired. He was convinced that this situation was the result of my father no longer being in charge of the furniture store. He never told me this, of course, but I guessed it from certain things he said, and I, out of respect for my father, didn't tell him the truth, that it had all started when Papá was still running the business, and if Jaime didn't know about it, it was because we hid it from him, afraid his fear would get the better of him and he'd quit.

I asked if Güero had come alone or with someone. He told me he'd come in alone, but the other guy waited outside.

"The tall one?"

"Yes."

Güero had promised me that he'd always come into the store by himself, leaving his sidekick outside. As long as he went along with that agreement, I knew they still respected me and that gave me some peace of mind. That's when the phone rang. It was Ofelia, who was calling to remind me, for the second time, about the lady in her Bible circle who was interested in buying a futon from our furniture store, and she gave me her name and number so I could call her. I wrote the number down again and promised I'd call without fail. Ofelia didn't know anything about Güero. It was a secret between me, my father, and Jaime. Between Jaime and me, rather, because I doubt my father would remember that arrangement. If she were to find out, my sister would have sold the furniture store without a second thought. She wanted to sell it anyway, because she said it wasn't a viable business anymore. I stood up and, moving away from the desk so Jaime wouldn't hear me, I asked if she thought Papá wrote poems.

"No, why?"

"I found one he'd written out by hand in an old furniture store account book. It came with the name of that poet, Isabel Fraire."

"She was his favorite poet. He must've copied it out."

"I know, but maybe he wrote poems, too."

I realized that both of us were talking about my father using the past tense—"he wrote," "she was his favorite poet"—as if he were dead.

"If Papá'd written any poems, we'd know," Ofelia said.

"I don't think so," I said.

"Why?"

"Because of how reserved he is. Papá doesn't know anyone."

"He knows a bunch of people," she said.

"I mean, he's never had a real friend."

"Neither have you."

"We're talking about him, not me," I exclaimed. "And you, who do you have? Father Clark?"

"I don't know what you have against Father Clark. If it weren't for him—"

"I'd be scrubbing toilets right now," I finished her sentence.

"Go to hell," she said, and hung up.

I looked at my watch. I was running late, and between one thing and another I forgot to call the futon lady for the second time.

———

I was late by the time I got to Margó Benítez's house; she was in a bad mood when she greeted me, but I don't know if it was because of my lack of punctuality or for some other reason. She instructed Aurelia to bring the coffee, gave me the Daphne du Maurier novel that was on the side table, and asked me to start reading.

"I brought a poem I'd like to read to you before I continue with the novel," I told her, and I opened my briefcase to take out the page where I'd copied Isabel Fraire's poem.

"Is it long?" she asked me.

"I don't know, it's a poem," and I showed her the page so she could decide for herself whether it was long or not. She noticed that it was written by hand and saw that it was my handwriting, which she recognized because I had to write the name of the person I visited and a brief summary of the reading on the visitation form she had to sign at the end of each session.

"Excuse me, Eduardo, I didn't know it was yours," she said.

"What?"

"You didn't tell me it's one of your poems. Go on, read it."

I looked at her, not knowing if I should tell her the truth or take advantage of the misunderstanding, which had suddenly softened her, making her look almost beautiful.

"It just came out, almost by accident," I said, giving in to the temptation to show off, and at that point Aurelia came in and leaned over with the coffeepot to fill our cups.

It seemed like she'd accentuated her inclination to expose her cleavage and Margó must've noticed the same thing because she told her rudely, "Leave the coffeepot here, I'll finish serving it."

The maid set the coffeepot on the side table and walked off, though not without smiling at me first.

"She does whatever she wants," Margó said quietly, serving the coffee, and she asked me to begin.

I'd practiced reading the poem and I read it without tripping up even once. I knew I'd impressed her because she held the cup of coffee in front of her mouth, not taking a single sip while I read, and when I finished she put it back on the saucer and said, "It's a magnificent poem. And you read poetry so differently from prose, Eduardo!"

"Of course, they're two different genres."

"I mean the delivery, the passion. When you read the novel it's obvious your head is somewhere else and you could care less about the story, but now that you've read the poem your attitude has changed completely. You really read it, and that's why I was so moved," and then she immediately added, "Drink your coffee, it's going to get cold. I can address you informally, use *tú*, can't I?"

"Yes, of course." I sipped my coffee and so did she, and we looked at each other again over our cups. I think I blushed, I set the cup on the saucer and picked up the book by Daphne du Maurier, opening it to the page where we'd left off. I asked her if she wanted me to start reading and she nodded. I read an entire page and had no idea what I'd read.

"Your head's in the clouds again," she said gently.

I closed the book and told her, "Yes, because the poem I just read to you isn't mine."

"Whose is it?"

"It's by Isabel Fraire, a Mexican poet, my father's favorite poet."

"Your father has good taste," she said.

"He's always said that she's the best poet in Mexico. I acted like a fool."

"Yes. Now keep reading."

"I didn't understand a thing I just read."

"Neither did I." And she laughed enthusiastically, and for the first time, the gloom the wheelchair imposed on her body parted and I had a glimpse of a desirable woman. Her laughter had disheveled her abundant black hair, usually tied back in a bun, giving her an aura of something between lascivious and unkempt that surprised me, and I asked if I could also use *tú* with her.

She took a sip of coffee and said, "You can't until you tell me what you did."

I asked her what she meant.

"Tell me why you were sentenced to a year of community service."

I briefly recounted what had happened. I was surprised that I didn't have any trouble doing so, even though it was the first time I'd told anyone. Other than the official court statements, I hadn't described the accident to anyone, not even Ofelia, and especially not to my father, who I wasn't sure even knew about it. Margó listened attentively, and when I finished, she called Aurelia to bring more coffee. The ugly and spirited maid arrived in no time, as if she were merely waiting for the order to appear, and she bowed dramatically as she refilled our cups, once again offering me a view of her stirring breasts, which seemed to be screaming to be tamed.

SINCE I NO LONGER used a car, my appreciation for traveling by foot had changed, and what before had struck me as an unreasonable distance now seemed perfectly feasible. Among the thousand horrendous things about the City of Eternal Spring, its public transportation took the cake. I discovered that most of the time I didn't need to use it if I simply modified my criteria regarding walkable distances, and that was one of the positive things the driving ban brought me.

When I left Margó Benítez's house I had plenty of
time before my appointment with Colonel Atarriaga,
and I remembered the Casa del Libro bookstore wasn't
far away. When I arrived, I was surprised by the change
the place had undergone. What had once been a real
bookstore was now a muddle of magazines, schoolbooks,
and home decorations. I went in and asked for the Daphne
du Maurier novel. They didn't have it, of course, but the
attendant suggested that I look for it in a used bookstore
that had just opened two blocks away. The news was
almost staggering, that a store selling used books had
opened in a city so devoid of such pleasant sanctuaries; I
thanked him, walked two blocks, and saw a sign with an
image of a snail on it, El Caracol, which I thought was a
promising name for a secondhand bookstore.

I was lucky, because they had the novel, though
not in a single volume; it was included in a collection
of the author's complete works. The store owner, a man
in his early sixties, graying and extremely agile, sold me
the book for two hundred pesos. I was already on the
street when I decided to go back and ask if he had any
books by Isabel Fraire. He studied me closely, I suppose
because he wasn't used to people asking for a book of
poetry, and he set off for a distant shelf, maneuvering
around several piles of books that blocked his way. He
came back holding a book in his hand, a green one.

"It's her collected poetry, if that helps. She just died,"
he informed me.

"When?"

"In April." And he added, "The cruelest month."

I had something to tell my father: His favorite poet had died. I asked the man how long he'd had the bookstore and he said two months. Now I understood why he was so energetic. His adventure was just beginning. I shook his hand as I said goodbye and went out to the street.

I had to hurry to make it to the Colonel's house on time. His single-story home was situated in the backyard of a larger house, where his landlords lived, and it was accessed by going down a long passageway through a door only he used. The entry was a little complicated. You had to ring a bell, the Colonel heard it, and, if he knew who it was, he'd go out to the patio and pull on a long cord that ran the length of the passageway and was attached to the door latch; otherwise, you had to wait for him to traverse the length of the corridor at his slow pace.

It was a dark, silent house. He greeted me with a subtle nod and sat in an armchair that had seen better days, ready to listen. I'd suggested that we read, taking into consideration his military past, *The Tartar Steppe* by Dino Buzzati, and he'd consented without question, as if he knew beforehand that sleep would overwhelm him after three or four pages. The book moved as slowly as he did, and I seriously doubted that he remembered what little he'd heard in previous sessions. When he closed his eyes, I continued reading for a while, then I closed the book and imitated him, surrendering as well to a brief nap.

It would have been super easy to steal whatever I wanted. I even knew where he kept his money, because one day we were interrupted by the landlord's maid, who'd come to collect the rent, and he, after closing the door halfway, went to a corner secretaire, opened one of the drawers, and took out a wad of bills, which he then handed to the maid; then he offered me an apology for the interruption and sat back down.

When I opened my briefcase to take out the Buzzati novel, the sheet with the Isabel Fraire poem fell to the floor; I picked it up and was going to put it away when it occurred to me I could read it to the Colonel.

"Do you like poetry?" I asked.

"Poetry?"

"Yes. Would you like me to read you a poem before we continue with the novel?"

"A poem!" he exclaimed, as if pondering some unfamiliar word.

"It's short," I clarified.

"How short?"

I held up the page. I felt like I was selling him something and regretted the idea immediately. All I needed was for him to complain to Father Clark, accuse me of forcing him to listen to poems he didn't like.

"Poems are dangerous," he said, smiling.

I smiled in turn, not knowing if he was joking or serious. I couldn't think of anything better to do than open the page, which was folded over, and read the first two lines to myself to see if they were dangerous or not.

"I think this one isn't," I said, feeling stupid.

"All of them are."

I should have asked him why he said that, but I didn't, and I thought that maybe his was an aversion that came from some deep hatred having to do with the same irregular form of the lines that must have seemed unreliable compared to the disciplined lines of prose. I folded the page and put it into my briefcase, took out the Buzzati book, looked for the page where we'd left off, and started to read. I saw him relax. It was obvious that he wasn't paying attention, that my voice was like background music. I wondered if he remembered my name, if he'd ever heard it.

I stopped reading when I heard him snoring. Maybe it was the way I didn't pay attention to what I read that made the Colonel sleepy. What was frustrating for Margó Benítez and what made the Jiménez brothers angry put the Colonel to sleep. But I had my reasons. Holding a book in front of someone staring at my lips, I couldn't help feeling like a preacher, and I was assaulted by the image of my sister reading the Bible to Celeste. That's why the meaning of words evaded me, and I only loaned them my voice, my "beautiful manly voice," as Father Clark had described it.

I opened my briefcase, making sure I didn't wake the Colonel, and took out the Isabel Fraire book I'd just bought. I looked at the title, which I hadn't noticed when I bought it: *Suspension Bridge: Collected Poems.* It seemed like an irrelevant title. Come on, all bridges are suspended, it's their central characteristic. I opened the book and didn't expect to see what I saw. The author had written a personal note in blue ink: "To Abigael Martínez, with gratitude and affection. Isabel Fraire." It was dated January 7, 2002, and the place wasn't specified, or maybe it was: "In this city of ours," it said. What city of ours? Mexico City? The City of Eternal Spring? Another city in the Mexican republic? It wasn't unusual to find books that had been signed and inscribed in used bookstores. I know because of my father, who hardly ever bought a book that wasn't used. With so much to read, he'd say, why waste your time on new books? He'd bring five or six home at a time, dusty and a little unsightly, and some were inscribed by the author or with the name of its previous owner written on the first page.

I had a little treasure in my hands to share with my father. Look, Papá, I'd say to him, I found a book by Isabel Fraire in a secondhand bookshop, with an inscription and everything. Was it possible that Papá knew Abigael Martínez? It was possible. When you live in a city as small and uncultured as this one, the few people who are fond of books tend to find each other.

What I was sure of is that Papá didn't know Isabel Fraire, and that it hadn't occurred to him that he could have known her. For all he knew, Isabel Fraire could have died thirty years ago or already have been dead when he'd started to read her poems.

I looked for the poem Papá'd copied in his ledger and I found it right away. I wondered if he'd copied it correctly, and since I had the page where I'd copied the poem to read to Margó, I took it out of my briefcase to compare it to the original. Papá'd copied it out perfectly, without adding or omitting anything, and that unfailing fidelity made me sad. I imagined him reproducing every one of the poem's words, trying not to make a mistake, doing so with the same apprehension that he received the merchandise delivered to the store from the capital or the provinces, careful it didn't hit a wall or collide with another piece of furniture. That's what his life had been like, taking care of things so they could pass from hand to hand, without becoming too attached to them and without interfering. On one occasion he'd told me, with a certain bit of pride, that among his friends when he was younger he was the only one who didn't drink very much, so when they went out he was in charge of getting all of them home, because most of the time they were drunk. I asked him if this role, a mixture of babysitter and watchman, bothered him, and he said it didn't, because being the only sober one, everyone confessed their peccadilloes and weaknesses to him, including the parents of his friends, who opened up to him when he'd deposit their kids safe and sound in their homes. I didn't find his explanation very convincing and he must've noticed because I saw his face turn gray, as if suddenly, after all those years, he understood that his friends had taken advantage of him or, even worse, that he'd assumed that custodial role out of cowardice, keeping the others from falling but at the price of never knowing what it was like to fall himself.

In essence, I read with the same spirit of detachment, that's why my eyes slid over the words, and now I wonder if all of this isn't related to the fact that we're a family of furniture sellers, accustomed to being detached from those things—tables, chairs, wardrobes— that for most people are an extension of their bodies. Mamá was the one who suffered most from that condition, because, especially at the beginning, she was in the habit of falling in love with pieces of furniture we were selling. She couldn't help it, even though she knew they were there to be sold and not to own. The piece she loved most was a slender sideboard made of reddish wood, with a double-doored glass display cabinet on top. We didn't have a sideboard in our house, and according to her, a house without a sideboard is not a respectable house. She shuddered every time a customer came into the store, afraid he'd buy it, because she hoped my father, seeing that we couldn't sell it, would decide to keep it. But my father stood his ground; we didn't have the money to hold on to a piece of furniture like that. He kept lowering the price, and every time he lowered it, Mamá cried, hiding in a corner or in one of the many alcoves and passageways that take shape in furniture stores as a result of the accumulation of furniture. When my father discovered there was another model of the same sideboard at a lower price, he had it delivered to the store and he placed it next to the other model on the floor, and that was all it took to dwindle Mamá's infatuation. When she saw that it was a mass-produced sideboard it lost all of its beauty for her. They both sold the same week and my mother never fell in love with another piece of furniture again.

The Colonel woke up half an hour later, signed the visitation form, and walked me to the door. Like always, when he shook my hand, he said, "Very good reading."

By the time I got home, Papá was already asleep, so I couldn't show him Isabel Fraire's book. I'd gotten used to not making any noise so I wouldn't wake him. Celeste and I would watch a few episodes of a program we liked, then she'd go to bed and I'd stay up to read. That night I told her I didn't feel like watching TV and went to my room to read *My Cousin Rachel*. I wanted to be familiar with the book I was reading to Margó Benítez. If I couldn't grasp the meaning of what I read in front of her, at least I could know what the book was about. It took me two hours to finish it, but when I turned out the light I was kept awake by the image of the older cousin

who uses her charm to entice young Philip to fall in love
with her. A marvelous woman, but at the same time the
cause of so much misfortune. Mostly it was her skin,
incredibly soft, that bewitched poor Philip, ten years her
junior, showing that poor provincial Englishman, who'd
never left his county, the overwhelming power a woman
can possess with her body. I wondered if Margó had
attempted to send me a message through that book; if
she identified with Rachel, the skilled woman, and saw
in me a copy of naïve Philip, whose spirit she was taking
it upon herself to refine and perfect or, worse, to subdue.

I SPENT THE MORNING in the furniture store,
working with Jaime to decide on the monthly sale prices.
We hadn't sold anything in ten days. We discounted
each piece of furniture, between ten and twenty percent,
depending on the item. It was one of the things I hated
most about that business: reducing the price of the
merchandise. Even if I wasn't born to run a business,
those moments of price adjustments stressed me out, and
I would have gladly left them in the hands of Jaime had I
not thought it was something only the owner should do,
if he doesn't want to lose his position of power over his
employees.

We wasted the entire morning affixing tags with a
suitable discount for each item, and we had an argument
about the Swiss bunk beds. Jaime was of the opinion

that twenty percent was appropriate, but I didn't agree; it was a select piece of furniture and therefore justified a smaller discount.

"We've had them for nearly a year," he argued.

He was right, but I didn't give in, and I told him to hang a ten percent tag on it. I wasn't blind to his look of disapproval, and for a brief moment I felt like firing him. I never found Jaime very pleasant anyway. Neither did my father. It was impossible to joke around with him. But he was efficient and honest, and he knew the furniture business better than anyone.

"If they don't sell this week, we'll put the twenty percent tag on them," I said in a conciliatory tone.

He wouldn't have said that. He shook his head, an indication of his disapproval, of condemnation.

"One doesn't play around with discounts," he said derisively. "You set the final discount once and for all, no matter what. Successive discounts make you look bad."

I didn't say anything. I knew he was right; I grabbed my jacket and hurried off to Sanborns de Piedra. I deserved it, after lowering prices and putting up with Jaime's sour face. When I arrived, I sat at one of the tables Gladis served and greeted her with a kiss on the cheek.

"The usual?"

I asked her about the stew and she made a subtle movement with her index finger to say I'd be better off skipping it.

"The usual then."

"Nene! A whole week and kiddo hasn't come around!" she scolded and went to the kitchen to turn in my order.

Luz Aurora, who served in another area, came to greet me with the same reproach: "We haven't seen you for a week, Nene. A lot of work at the furniture store?"

"I wish it were that," I said. "It's a shitty time right now, no one has any money."

She took a five-hundred-peso note out of her pocket and gave it to me. "Thanks, Nene. It took me a while, but here it is."

I took the money and asked her about Tristana.

"She called in sick again. One of these days they're going to fire that girl."

The girl in question, Tristana, another one of the waitresses, was sixty-five years old. Luz Aurora went back to her tables, kissing my cheek as she said goodbye.

The nickname, Nene, came from my father, who'd been a regular at Sanborns de Piedra, even when Mamá was alive. He'd take us there on Sunday mornings for breakfast and several of these waitresses had watched me grow up.

I wasn't the only regular. There was El Conde, the Count, who greeted my father from afar when they happened to see each other in the restaurant, though they never spoke a word to each other. I'd inherited that custom and I greeted him the same way. He was a small, nervous man, married to an elegant woman, also small, who seemed unhappy and sometimes came out for breakfast with him, though neither of them spoke to each other during the entire meal. The peculiar thing about El Conde was that, despite his advanced age and short stature, he rode a Harley-Davidson. He'd leave his helmet and gloves on the table, in view of everyone, and I suppose he went to Sanborns so everyone would know that he owned a powerful motorcycle. One day he asked me, through Gladis, to loan him two thousand pesos. He was sitting on the far side of the café, Gladis informed me of his request, and I got up and went to the ATM, which was at the restaurant's exit. I withdrew the two thousand pesos and gave them to Gladis, who then walked over and gave them to El Conde. He made a gesture of gratitude from his table, to which I responded with another gesture. A week later, once again through Gladis, he paid his debt, including a box of chocolates with the money. We nodded from our tables and when El Conde left the establishment, I called Gladis over and gave her the chocolates, a gift for her grandchildren.

Because the Valverde Furniture Store had been in the city for more than twenty years, many assumed we were rich. Maybe we had been at some point, without realizing, but that ended with the huge influx of ready-to-assemble furniture that was sold in the discount stores, which dealt a heavy blow to the traditional furniture stores like ours.

My sister was right. It was no longer a worthwhile business. Jaime was the problem. Paying off his pension was going to cost us a fortune. We'd have to wait for a good run before we could sell the store, that was my policy, though I was the first to recognize that it wasn't a policy but a way to postpone a traumatic decision.

Gladis arrived with my Swiss enchiladas and asked about my father.

"Still going," I told her. "I had a ramp installed where the stairs connect the living room with the rest of the house so he can use his wheelchair to go from his room to the porch and get a little sun."

I took out my cell phone and showed her a series of pictures I'd taken of the ramp, but I forgot that there was one of my father in his wheelchair among them. When Gladis saw him the color drained from her face. She hadn't seen him in more than a year. Her expression showed me the magnitude of my father's decline, and though she didn't tell me that he was unrecognizable, that was the word on the tip of her tongue. I felt awful showing her my father's physical ruin. It was unfair to him and, because I caught her off guard, to her too.

"He's so thin!" she said, returning my cell phone, and for the first time our repertoire of jokes wasn't enough to maneuver us around that low point.

"It's no way to live," was all I could think to say to her, and she rushed to wait on a customer who was calling her from another table.

———

THE RESÉNDIZES were my most well-to-do hosts.
They had a two-story house with a spacious yard, two
maids, and an elegant car, which was strange because
the home reading program had been created for the
elderly or infirm with limited resources. They were the
only ones who clapped when I finished reading. They
praised my voice like no one else and Doña Reséndiz
asked me once if I sang. Only in the shower, I answered.
You have the voice of a tenor, she said, and Señor
Reséndiz, who agreed with everything his wife said,
nodded his head. They didn't make any comments about
the book we'd read. We'd started off reading Kafka's
Metamorphosis, but in the third session they asked if we
could change to something less depressing. I suggested
Capote's *Breakfast at Tiffany's*. At the end of the reading
they gave me a round of applause, and when I asked
if they liked the new book, they answered in unison,
"It's interesting." I realized that they hadn't liked it and
the following week I read them a short story by Agatha
Christie. After their applause I asked what they'd
thought.

"It's an entertaining novel," Amalia Reséndiz said. "Is
it very long?"

"It isn't a novel, it's a story, and we finished it," I
answered.

"I like it very much," she said. "What about you,
dear?"

"Me, too," her husband answered.

Unlike Margó Benítez and the Jiménez brothers, who criticized me for not paying attention to what I read, the Reséndizes only seemed to notice my voice which, if I didn't want to disappoint them, forced me to put a lot of effort into my pronunciation. I was more exhausted from these readings than when I left the Vigils' house. My fear of letting the Reséndizes down and their concentrated attention on the sound of my voice put me in a situation much like that of a stage actor. I hated the bond that had formed between me and the old married duo, but their applause and the sincere admiration I read in their eyes when I closed the book gave me something like the elation an actor or singer must feel when he is given a standing ovation.

One afternoon they asked if they could invite a couple of friends to my next reading. They said it like that, "your next reading," as if it were a *performance*. I consented, and when I arrived at their house I saw that the couple of friends was not one couple but in fact three and that they were dressed rather formally. By chance, I was too because I'd come from a wake and hadn't had time to go home to change my clothes. When Doña Amalia opened the door and saw me in a suit, she hugged me enthusiastically, believing I'd dressed up for the occasion deliberately. It didn't matter that I'd told her I'd come from a wake.

"No, no, you look amazing!" she said, now using *tú* instead of addressing me formally, and she introduced

me to her friends with these words: "Our artist has
arrived."

In a way, that was the word that determined the
course of subsequent events. Had I known, I would have
left their house at that exact moment, giving as a pretext
some physical malaise, and on my next visit I would have
asked them to never invite anyone again.

Amalia Reséndiz's guests shook my hand with a
degree of deference, and what was supposed to be a
friendly and intimate gathering turned into a small
theatrical production. Amalia had found another Agatha
Christie story, which I doubt very much she had taken
the time to read. When I read it out loud I concentrated
on the inflection of the words, hardly understanding
the story at all, and after the reading, which was well-
applauded, the owners of the house insisted that I join
them for a light refreshment of wine and sandwiches.

The special evening, the soiree as Amalia Reséndiz
liked to call it, was repeated the following week. Doña
and Señor Reséndiz took for granted that I'd love to
repeat the experience and Amalia Reséndiz called me
the night before to tell me three other couples were
joining them and, in passing, she congratulated me on
my cashmere suit, in which I "looked splendid." The
next day, when I was leaving the house in the same suit,
Celeste asked where I was going dressed so elegantly
and I said to a wake. I made the mistake of wearing the
same tie, something that my host didn't overlook, and

after hugging me said in a flirtatious voice while she straightened the knot, "Hmmm, I've seen this beautiful tie before," and, turning to her guests, exclaimed, "Our artist has arrived!"

There were a dozen guests and the old married duo had a hard time finding seats for everyone. Being by far the youngest person at the event, I had to help Señor Reséndiz bring an armchair down from a second-floor bedroom. In the end I had to carry it myself because the old man gave up halfway down the staircase.

"Our athlete has arrived!" Amalia Reséndiz exclaimed when she saw me entering the room carrying the armchair, and I loathed her.

I hadn't brought another story by Agatha Christie. At first I thought I'd bring a few humorous texts by Jorge Ibargüengoitia, another one of my father's favorite authors, but when I started to practice them, I realized that if you're going to read something funny you need to be immersed in it completely in order to provide the correct situational tone. So, because of my inability to understand what I was reading, I threw that idea out. After a lot of thought I decided on a few poems by Isabel Fraire. I'd never read any poems in that house and Isabel Fraire's weren't exactly the "Nocturne for Rosario" type, but I told myself that these people wanted to hear my beautiful voice, not understand what they heard, and it was a wise decision, because the reading was a resounding success. I read with feeling; Margó Benítez, who'd been surprised by how my reading style had changed when I read poems, was right. I felt strangely free to immerse myself in the whimsical typography of Isabel Fraire's lines, which seemed to be broken, mimicking the irregular breath of a pedestrian in one of our cities. The feeling of disorientation I felt even before I read them seemed familiar because of the way they were scattered across the page. I felt like this was my life since the accident, or the misfortune, as Celeste called it: something whole made up of fragments that were waiting for an opportunity to come together again.

"You made me cry," Amalia Reséndiz whispered in my ear when I finished reading, and added, "I'm going to give you a pair of neckties that will enhance your face."

WE FINALLY SOLD the Swiss bunk beds on Monday. I was in the furniture store when the young couple came in. Because I'm quite a bit younger than Jaime, they thought he was the owner and I the employee; the same thing had happened before. They were straightforward with me and I had no problem closing the deal. I was happy with the sale and that I'd showed Jaime that we could sell the bunk beds at only a ten percent discount.

Güero came to the furniture store that afternoon, when I wasn't there, and left word with Jaime that he needed to talk to me. Jaime called to let me know and told me that Güero would be waiting for me at Sanborns de Piedra at five o'clock, near the bar.

I arrived on time. At that hour the bar's deserted so I sat at the most secluded table and ordered a beer. I really wanted a gin and tonic but a strong drink encourages certain intimacy, and if there was something I didn't want it was to cozy up to Güero. Besides, I was going to foot the bill. He arrived ten minutes later, when I'd almost finished my beer. I realized that I hadn't seen him for some time, because he'd aged; I didn't tell him this of course, because that's something friends say to each other.

"Been a long time!" he said almost without looking at me.

The waiter approached to take his order, but I beat him to it: "The same for the señor." I wanted to make it clear that I wasn't there to buy him drinks but to talk business and then leave.

"You could have at least let me pick the beer. I don't like Indio," he said.

"What do you want?"

"A León, if they have it."

The waiter came with the Indio.

"Bring the señor a León and I'll keep the Indio," and I swallowed the last of my other beer so the man could take the bottle with him. Then, facing Güero, who was looking around the room, which is what he always did, I asked what this meeting was about.

"I'll wait for my beer, give me a break, man."

"I don't have time; I have to be somewhere else in an hour."

It was true. I had a reading in Colonel Atarriaga's house and I had my briefcase with me.

"They told me about your misfortune," Güero said, using Celeste's expression. "I'm sorry."

"It was an accident," I said.

"An unfortunate accident."

The waiter came with the León, asked if we needed anything else, and I said no. Güero took a long drink from his beer, wiped his lips with a napkin, and told me that he was in trouble. Someone had robbed him, taken the envelope with our money inside. At first he thought he'd dropped it in a taxi, but later he realized he'd been robbed at the seafood restaurant where he met with some childhood buddies, and he could swear that one of them had taken it.

Here, had we been friends, I would have said, "Those are some great buddies you've got!" But we weren't, and I held my tongue. Then he told me that he had to turn in the invoice the next day, and I was struck by the word "invoice," a tidy cloak concealing his criminal behavior.

"And?" I asked him, looking him in the eyes for the first time. Until then, each of us focusing on our beers, we'd avoided looking at each other.

"I need you to loan me that money, or else..." and he pulled his index finger across his neck, a gesture with a clear meaning.

"Are you threatening me?"

"You don't get it, the one whose neck is on the line is me. They know Jaime gave me the envelope because David was outside the store."

"David's the tall one?"

"Yes. Forget his name, I shouldn't have told you and it's not going to help you any by knowing his name." He drained what was left of his beer in one gulp and I realized that he was terrified.

"Want another one?" I asked.

He said he did. I waved to the waiter, who rushed over, and I ordered another León. Güero thanked me.

"Even if I wanted to, I don't have that kind of money," I told him.

"Do everything you can to get it. I'll pay you back, little by little. I promise."

The absurdity of the situation wasn't lost on me. The extortioner asking for a loan from the one he was shaking down, and I wondered if he'd noticed the same thing.

"Why me, exactly?" I asked.

"Because you're the only decent person I can ask for help."

"You're the one who decided to surround himself with a bunch of brutes."

The waiter brought his beer and took away our empty bottles. Güero looked at me with determination.

"Eduardo," he said, "I won't call myself a saint because I've never been one. Your father knew that when

I asked him for work, and still he hired me. He saved my life. I only want to tell you that it upsets me to be taking money from you. Not a day goes by that I don't think about that, and Guiomar still hasn't forgiven me. If she worships anyone, it's your father. But if I wasn't around, things would be a lot worse for you."

"I know that tune."

"Unfortunately, I don't know any other," he replied. "When I heard they'd set their sights on the furniture store, I stepped forward. I was the one who told them, 'Let's go for the Valverdes.' Do you think you would've been spared? Now, instead of dealing with me, you'd be dealing with David, and you don't know these people, you don't know what they're capable of."

"So, I should thank you," I blurted out.

Had this been a Hollywood movie, I would have stood up at this point and, after throwing a bill on the table, walked out. But instead of Hollywood we were in the City of Eternal Spring, and the thug in front of me wasn't Robert De Niro but Güero, the first employee to work for us in the furniture store, and he was scared to death.

I nodded for the waiter to bring me the bill. I had to be at the Colonel's house in half an hour. While I waited, I did some quick calculations. Only a small portion of Papá's savings was available, and it was just half the amount Güero needed. The rest was locked in and wouldn't be available for another three days. I only had a quarter of the total amount he needed. The other quarter was still missing. Asking Ofelia for it was out of the question, because then I'd have to tell her that Güero, Guiomar's husband, was blackmailing us. I thought of the old Reséndiz couple, but if Father Clark found out that I'd asked them to loan me money, he'd kick me out of the program and I'd end up cleaning toilets in the public hospital or in some prison.

"So how about it?" Güero asked me.

"I can't give you an answer right now. Call Jaime tomorrow morning, early, and he'll let you know."

He stood up, not sure whether to shake my hand or not. He decided not to, and said suddenly, as if he'd rehearsed the phrase in front of a mirror, "If Guiomar hasn't gone to see your father, it's because she's dying of embarrassment."

I paid the bill the waiter brought over and waited a few minutes to give Güero time to walk away. I left the bar and headed toward the cash register. I looked for Gladis. When she saw me, she started walking in my direction. I indicated that I was in a hurry, blowing her a kiss as I reached the exit. I stopped there. What if I asked her for the money? I knew she wouldn't hesitate to give it to me, but I imagined coming to Sanborns carrying that debt, no longer free to order a moderately expensive dish or overpriced beer. It wasn't just that. She'd seen me loan money to El Conde and Luz Aurora; she knew that if she needed it, she could depend on me and that made me look really good. I was Nene, and if I asked her for money, I'd become an adult, like El Conde. I'd rather confront David. Because it was clear that if Güero didn't turn the famous invoice over to his bosses, they'd get rid of him without a second thought and from then on I'd have to deal directly with the tall one.

It was getting dark by the time I got to the Colonel's house. The weather was starting to change and he'd put on a sweater and a pair of lined house slippers. True to form, he didn't offer me anything. We sat in our respective places and I pulled *The Tartar Steppe* out of my briefcase, cleared my throat, and began to read. Every so often I'd look up to see if he'd closed his eyes. He took longer than usual to do so. Maybe he sensed something. When he fell asleep, I didn't trust myself and kept reading for a while longer. Only when I heard his gentle snoring did I close the book; I got up and walked to the secretaire. My heart was pounding. I opened the first drawer on the left where there were a few pens and an eraser; I opened the one below, which was empty; in the third, which was in the middle and the largest of the three, there was a bundle of black-and-white photographs held together by an elastic band. When I turned it over I saw the wad of bills. My fingers were trembling, and I looked at the Colonel, who continued snoring, and I kept looking at him as I removed the money. I wasn't sure if I should count it right there or go back to the armchair; I decided to return to the armchair, lifted the briefcase from the floor and opened it on my knees, removed the elastic band to separate the cash from the pictures, and counted the money. It was a little more than what I needed so I took just enough, which I put in one of the compartments; I gathered the rest of the cash with the pictures, closed the briefcase, and went back to the secretaire to put the bundle in the drawer. When I sat back down, it took forever for my heart to recover its normal rhythm.

That night, when I opened the briefcase in my room to take out the money, I saw a picture of the Colonel among the cash, which must have been separated from the others, and such carelessness on my part put me in a rotten mood. The Colonel was dressed like a civilian, hugging a much younger woman, there was some kind of establishment in the background that could have been a hotel or spa. Judging by the Colonel's appearance, the picture must have been taken ten years ago. I put it in one of the briefcase compartments thinking that I'd return it when I went back to his house to replace the money.

The next day, first thing, I went to the bank and withdrew the money that wasn't tied up in Papá's fixed-term account, then I went to Rosario's cubicle to say hello and asked if I could take a picture of her with my phone because my father would love to have a picture of her. She told me that, for security reasons, no one was allowed to take pictures inside the bank, but we could take one outside, and she asked me to wait for a few minutes because she needed to make a call. There was a wooden bench outside the bank, and I waited for her there. After twenty minutes I got up, thinking she'd forgotten about the picture, but I didn't have the nerve to go in and remind her. She was the branch director and maybe something important had happened. I sat back down. Another twenty minutes passed. After an hour I got up and left. Certainly, something unexpected had come up, but the thing left a bad taste in my mouth. Work came first, but was it such a big deal to step outside for one minute?

My cell phone rang. It was Jaime. He told me Güero was going to swing by the furniture store in half an hour "to see if I'd come up with what we agreed on." Since I didn't want to see him, I took a taxi to get to the furniture store as quickly as possible and leave the money with Jaime. When I arrived, instead of putting the cash in an envelope like I did with the money for the protection fee, I wound the bills into a crude roll and bound it with a rubber band, to make it clear to Güero (and to Jaime, and to myself) that one thing had nothing to do with the other.

"Something special," I said to Jaime, giving him the roll of cash.

"And the other isn't?" he replied sarcastically, and I was a hairbreadth from telling him to go to hell, but luckily I contained myself, because if I fired him, I knew the store would fall apart.

I walked out and stopped the first taxi I saw.

"Sanborns de Piedra," I ordered the driver, and I repeated it to myself, like a prayer: *Sanborns de Piedra, Sanborns de Piedra*. It was the only place in that city where I felt comfortable. When I arrived, I looked for Gladis. Then I remembered it was Tuesday morning, the shift she had off. I sat where I always do and an extremely tall young woman who'd been working there a few months came to wait on me. Gladis knew how I liked my rolls: hot, with a little butter and without flattening them out on the griddle. I gave the same instructions to the tall lady and pulled the Isabel Fraire book out of my backpack.

I hadn't slept well, thinking about Colonel Atarriaga, who could realize at any moment that the money had gone missing from his secretaire. This whole time I had another prayer in my mouth, that he wouldn't have to open that little piece of furniture until the next day when I could return the money I'd taken. I bet on my luck: if the tall lady brought me flat rolls, the Colonel was going to discover he'd been robbed; if she brought fluffy ones, I was safe. The tall lady came out of the kitchen carrying the tray on her shoulder and approached my table, walking with what I imagined was a North African cadence. I've always liked tall women. They're more sensitive and loyal than shorter women, and if they're ugly, they aren't completely ugly because their height helps dilute their shortcomings. The opposite is also

true, and it's rare to see a really beautiful tall woman,
but I think moderate beauty is better than the irresistible
kind, if the latter comes accompanied with malice.

Mireya, that's what was written on the tall lady's
name tag, opened the tray stand, set the tray down,
lifted off the heat cover, and set the plate in front of me.
I looked at the rolls, I looked at her, and I didn't move.

"Señorita, I told you I didn't want the rolls flattened
out."

"You said a little butter, señor."

"And without flattening them on the griddle. It was
the first thing I told you."

"Do you want me to take them back?"

"Please."

She took the rolls, leaving me engulfed in a
foreboding fog. If Ofelia hadn't been so stubborn, I
thought. If she'd had a little common sense, she'd have
understood that our deal with Güero was the modus
vivendi of a large part of the city's businesses. I'd have
asked her for the money, instead of stealing it from
Colonel Atarriaga, and I wouldn't be steps away from
ending up in jail. I corrected myself: It wasn't stealing,
because I was going to return his five thousand pesos the
next day, immediately after withdrawing the money from
the bank. How I was going to do that, I still didn't know.

Mireya came back with fresh, fluffy rolls. They
weren't flat, I thanked her and watched her walk away.
I'd lost my appetite and I no longer felt like reading

Isabel Fraire's poems. It was a cool, sunny morning, one of those befitting that odious nickname, City of Eternal Spring. I was lost in thought while my rolls and coffee got cold, and Mireya noticed.

"Something wrong with the rolls, señor?"

"No, they're fine. I lost my appetite."

"Sometimes that happens," she said and walked away with a camel-like gait. Then these lines of poetry I'd read a while back came to mind: "There are avenues so wide / that crossing them is another avenue." I couldn't remember if I'd read them in one of Papá's notebooks where he'd copied them out by hand or somewhere else. Maybe they weren't even part of a poem but a phrase I'd read or heard in some advertisement.

If we had lived in a better world, I would have asked Mireya, "Hey, Mireya, I just remembered these lines from a poem: 'There are avenues so wide / that crossing them is another avenue.' Do you know who wrote them?"

"Of course: that's Iván Buruskov, the Ukrainian poet, from his book *The Deadly Dahlias*, published in 1964; José Emilio Pacheco's Spanish translation is excellent. How are those rolls?"

"Everything's great, thanks Mireya."

But this was not a better world, it was the City of Eternal Spring, a city that had no soul, only swimming pools, as my father used to say. I took a sip of coffee, opened the packet of jam so I could spread it on the rolls, and when I looked up I saw Father Clark come

in accompanied by a woman. They looked around for
a table. So they wouldn't see me, I crouched down to
pick something nonexistent off the floor, spent twenty
seconds looking at my shoes, straightened up again, and
just then, the priest saw me. He waved, led the woman
to a table, and then came over to mine.

"I am glad to see you, Eduardo, I was hoping to have
a word with you," he told me, using *tú* with me for the
first time and extending his hand. I stood up to shake
his hand and he sat down without asking permission,
pointing at my chair for me to sit, as if it were his table
and not mine, and he told me that the Jiménez brothers
would be expecting me the following morning at eleven
to finish my reading, as we'd agreed. I told him I was
surprised that they'd have scheduled me at that hour,
because we always saw each other in the afternoon.

"They has the higher hands," he said.

"Have the upper hand," I corrected.

"Are you going to take someone as a witness?" He
ignored my correction.

I told him I was thinking of taking Celeste, my
father's caretaker.

"That seems reasonable to me."

He continued to look at me as if he'd just discovered
the resemblance between me and Ofelia. Mireya came
over with a menu; he told her he was sitting at another
table and asked if they had machaca con huevos, to
which Mireya replied yes.

"I am glad," he said. "The other Sanborns hardly ever has it," but he didn't specify which Sanborns, only said the "other," though I knew it was the one on Plan de Ayala, because Ofelia had eaten there with him.

Mireya poured me more coffee and I said, "This is the best Sanborns in the city. They make the best rolls," and I added, glancing at Mireya, "In the other ones they flatten them on the griddle, and they remove the crunchy bits."

She walked away with her pot of coffee.

"I do not like rolls," Father Clark said.

I looked at his eyes. They were the most impenetrable eyes I'd ever seen, and I thought they could hide as much from a saint as from a murderer. He looked at me as if he were still assessing how I resembled my sister, which made me think that maybe he was in love with her, too.

To pull him out of that trance, I said, "Ofelia really admires you."

"We are good friends."

"I know, and you're also her confessor."

"Yes."

Since I didn't say anything, he asked me, "Do you think one cannot be friend and confessor at the same time?"

I thought, because of a certain tremble in his voice, that yes, he was in love with her.

"No," I answered.

"If we accept that a confessor is as weak as those who confess to him, friendship is perfectly possible, no?"

It sounded like a prepared response.

"Say it like that and it certainly sounds very lovely," I said, "but in practice, the one who listens to the sins of others acquires an unquestionable authority over them."

"Do you think I am in a position of authority over your sister?"

"Yes."

I was about to ask if he was in love with Ofelia. He'd have said no, and he'd have thought I was stupid for asking. But he must have read that question in my eyes, because he lost his poise and looked over my shoulder, probably looking for the woman he'd come in with.

"It is a matter of debate, but they are waiting for me," he said, standing up and making the chair wobble, almost tipping it over. Apparently, he had problems getting up.

"Ah, I forgot," he exclaimed. "Colonel Atarriaga called me earlier today. Do not get up." I had stood up abruptly when I heard the Colonel's name. "He told me that you forgot your umbrella at his house last night."

I'd forgotten it on purpose, to have an excuse to return the following day.

"Good, I thought I'd lost it," I said uncertainly.

"He said to tell you to pick it up anytime you want."

I thanked him, we shook hands, and while I watched him walk away, I felt my pulse pounding in my temples.

The Colonel, apparently, had not yet noticed that he was missing five thousand pesos.

The news brought back my appetite and I sat down to eat my rolls. When I finished, I asked for the check. While I waited my turn to pay at the cash register, I looked in the direction where Father Clark was seated. The woman with him was blond, good-looking, older, about Ofelia's age. He was gesticulating, and the woman was looking at him, visibly impressed. I thought that, like her and Ofelia, there must be other women who invited him out for breakfast, and that he charmed them all with his flashy manners. Perhaps in some cases the breakfast or lunch was a preamble to something else. I never would have condemned him for that. It was likely that he, with his bearlike vigor, could provide these women more pleasure and affection than their conventional husbands. Suddenly I had the feeling that we were alike and that deep down he abhorred his celestial eyes, which had opened so many doors for him, of course, but none of the ones he wished had opened. Perhaps he'd scrutinized me a few minutes earlier because he saw in me someone who'd drifted off course, and that reminded him of the deeper meaning of his vocation, which he'd lost in the slightly frivolous circle in which he now moved, surrounded by ladies who held him in such high esteem.

I decided to walk home, and after a few blocks I stopped, opened my backpack, took out Isabel Fraire's book, and reread the words she'd written in her inscription: "In this city of ours." Was it possible Isabel Fraire had felt like the City of Eternal Spring was hers? I wasn't far from El Caracol bookstore, so I decided to go there. I was sweating when I arrived because the last stretch of street was on an incline. There was only one customer, flipping through a book at the back of the store. The owner, as usual, was flitting from one side of the store to the other, and when he saw me, he came up to ask what I was looking for. He'd recognized me.

I took out Fraire's book and opened it to the first page: "I found this dedication in the book I bought from you the other day."

He looked at the dedication, nodded, and told me that he couldn't exchange the book because it was the only copy he had.

"I don't want to exchange it," I told him, "I was just curious if by chance you know the person she'd inscribed it for."

"Abigael Martínez?"

"Yes."

"That's me."

I looked at him, felt stupid, and closed the book.

"I'm asking because Isabel Fraire is my father's favorite poet and I thought that by chance he and the person she inscribed it to knew each other."

He asked me what my father's name was. I told him, and I handed him my card from the furniture store. He looked at it and said that he didn't have the pleasure of knowing my father, though he knew about the furniture store because he walked by it sometimes. I told him I didn't want to keep the copy the author had inscribed for him and that I'd give it back if he could get me another copy of the same book.

"It doesn't matter, you can keep it," he replied, and I thought he must have been in serious financial trouble if he'd sold a book signed by the author, who also happened to be a friend of his.

I put the book in my backpack and told him, "In any case, if you get another copy, let me know; you can keep my card."

He took the card and asked me where my father had met Isabel Fraire.

"He hasn't met her," I told him, and added: "My father doesn't know anyone." He looked at me, as if waiting for me to add something after such a lapidary statement, and then I said, "He's sick and I run the furniture store now. The worst thing for him is that he can't read anymore."

"Why don't you read to him?"

That hadn't occurred to me. I was a reader in seven different homes, and I'd never read even one page to my father.

"I'm not very good at reading out loud," I said to justify myself. "I can't seem to get interested in what I read."

"The same thing happened to me. It happened to me with Isabel, in fact."

"You read to her?"

"She came to spend the weekend with us, fell off
a ladder, and broke a leg. She was in the hospital for
two weeks, unable to move. My wife visited her in the
mornings and I went in the afternoons, and since I'm
not very talkative, I read her a novel. But I read poorly, I
got bored and I bored her, so one afternoon she said we
should forget about the novel and I should read recipes
from a cookbook one of the nurses had loaned her. I
enjoyed them and so did she. And after the recipes we
moved on to poems, which are similar."

"How are they similar?" I asked him.

"They're recipes for life, let's say, and even though
we might not like the dish they describe, we admire
how well they describe it. All the pleasure in poetry is in
that."

I nodded, though not very convinced, and I asked if
Isabel Fraire came to the City of Eternal Spring often.

"She'd show up suddenly," he answered. "She'd come
to see someone, we never asked who it was, and she
never told us. Do you want to look at the poetry section?"

I told him I didn't have time right then, but that I'd
be back on another occasion. We shook hands and I
was about to ask what city the words "this city of ours"
referred to but I lost my nerve. Who was I to stick my
nose into other people's dedications?

When I got home, Papá was asleep, as usual. He
slept in his room, he slept in front of the TV, and he

slept on the porch when Celeste took him out for a little sun after breakfast. The cancer was gnawing away at him, was consuming more and more of his substance every day, but it respected his sleep. Maybe everything had become a dream for him, as a way to protect himself from the disease.

I went to my room, opened the notebook I use to record the furniture store deposits and expenses, and wrote on the last page: "My father doesn't know anyone." It was the second time that phrase had materialized on my lips, and I thought it was a line of poetry, that's why I wrote it down. I'd never written a poem and I didn't intend to start now, but I thought that, being a line of poetry, I should write it down. I had no idea what line could follow, one similarly categorical or one that spelled things out. Poetry is so difficult; the world must be full of first lines like mine, which launched a poetic career while at the same time bringing it to a close.

I asked Celeste where she kept the two or three cookbooks she'd look through, to savor their pictures mostly and sometimes to make a recipe with my help, and Ofelia's. She went to the credenza in the living room and brought them to me. There was a little book of recipes for Italian pasta dishes and one for Mexican Christmas cuisine. I sat on the porch and carefully read three ravioli recipes: al pesto, alla puttanesca, and with marinara sauce. I didn't find them at all enjoyable. It wasn't any better with the Mexican Christmas cuisine,

where I got lost in the process of making romeritos
a la jaliciense. I closed both books and left them on
the folding table, thinking that Abigael Martínez was
mistaken. Poems are not like recipes, because recipes
only make sense taken as a whole, unlike poems which
can be read in fragments, without the obligation
of finishing them; one could stop halfway through,
fascinated by four or five lines and reread them countless
times, forgetting about the poem as a whole. At least
that's how a lot of people read poetry. But with a recipe
you have to read the whole thing, because the dish
won't turn out or it won't be any good if you stop in
the middle.

I called Celeste and told her she should talk to her
niece about filling in for her the following day, because I
needed her to help me with several errands, among them
visiting Señor Ventriloquist. Again she asked me if she
had to dress up and I said no.

That night Papá couldn't sleep and wanted to get up.
I was afraid that the metastasis in his bones had started
its difficult demolition work and that this waking in the
middle of the night was the prologue to his suffering,
which Celeste and I were expecting, dreading, from
one day to the next. Fortunately, in this instance, it only
seemed to be a nightmare. Celeste made him some
jasmine tea and then she went back to bed and I stayed
with him. I made another cup of tea for myself, pushed
his wheelchair up to the dining-room table, and sat

beside him. For a long time neither of us spoke. When I told him I'd bought a book by Isabel Fraire, he nodded his head; I asked if he wanted to see it and he said yes.

I went to my room and returned with the book, he opened it, looked at the inscription, and said, "It's dedicated."

"Yes."

"How kind. Thank her for me. How is she?"

I took off my glasses and cleaned them with a napkin.

"Good, she sends her regards. It's a collection of her poems."

He nodded and started to flip through the pages. I was watching him to see if he recognized the poems he'd read so many times before. Suddenly his face lit up and, smiling, he read out loud: "Your skin, like sheets of sand and sheets of water swirling." He put the book on the table and, without looking, he continued: "Your skin, with its louring mandolin brilliance. / Your skin, where my skin arrives as if coming home / and lights a silenced lamp. / Your skin, that...that..."

He searched his memory for the next words. I picked up the book to help him, looked for the line, and said, "Your skin that nourishes..." and he remembered: "Your skin that nourishes my eyes." But he hesitated again, looked at me impatiently, and I told him the beginning of the next line: "and wears my name..."

"Ah, yes, 'and wears my name like a new dress.'"

He looked at me again. His eyes, like those of a castaway on the verge of sinking, looking at the one next to him, waiting for him to help. I told him: "Your skin a mirror . . . where my skin . . ."

"Where my skin," he repeated, and repeated again, "Where my skin . . ."

"Recognizes me," I finished the line.

Something inside him pulled away sharply, I saw it in his gaze. He refused to continue remembering and fixed his eyes on his cup of tea. That poem, which he'd squirreled away in his memory for years, had now become unfamiliar. "Take me to bed," he said brusquely.

I obeyed and helped him lie down; I went back to the dining room to turn out the lights and then went to my room. Abigael Martínez was right, poems are a whole, like recipes; you can't read them halfway through or recite a few lines, you have to take them as seriously as the poet who wrote them and who fought all the way to the last line before stopping. The fact that he remembered a few lines of a poem didn't attenuate my father's frustration; it would have been better to remember none of them at all. He knew that he'd just lost something that had always been part of him, in its complete and living entirety, and he must have felt like a useless old man.

Celeste and I arrived at the bank five minutes before it opened. Rosario hadn't arrived yet. Mario, the

manager in the adjoining cubicle, stood up obsequiously
and asked how he could help me. I explained what I
needed to do, and I introduced him to Celeste. She, even
though I'd told her otherwise, had dressed up as formally
as she could, donning a silk shawl from India that Ofelia
had given her for Christmas, which made her look like
a cross between a Tehuana and a palm reader. We sat
down, and Mario had the money order ready in less than
ten minutes. I went to the bank teller and when I came
back to the cubicle, Celeste was holding Mario's left hand
between both of hers and she was rubbing his wrist.

"When you wake up and when you go to bed," she
was explaining to him.

"Where can I find the ointment you mentioned?"
Mario asked her.

"You won't find it in the pharmacies. I have it sent
from my hometown. Señor Eduardo can bring you a
bottle when he comes back."

Mario glanced at me appreciatively and I smiled
back at him, despite myself. Celeste stood up, the two
kissed goodbye on the cheek, and we left the bank. On
the street, Celeste told me that the young man had a
tendinitis problem resulting from his excessive use of
the computer mouse. I was annoyed by the way she was
drawing on my time without consulting me first, but
I didn't complain to her about it, because now I had
the perfect excuse to come back to the bank and take
Rosario's picture for my father.

I hailed a cab as soon as we got to the Avenida. It was one of the few virtues of the City of Eternal Spring: There were more taxis than flies. If you raised your hand to sneeze, a taxi stopped in front of you. I gave the driver the name of the street where Colonel Atarriaga lived, and during the trip Celeste extolled, for the taxi driver, the benefits of the ointment she'd just prescribed to Mario. I don't remember how she managed to introduce the topic. I noticed that she became more loquacious on the street. Perhaps the temporary separation from my father infused her with energy. The taxi driver had a problem like Mario's, not in the wrist but in his neck, and when he asked Celeste where he could procure the ointment, she told him that she has it sent from her hometown.

"I'm taking a small bottle to Señor Mario this week; he works at the Banorte branch where you, señor, picked us up, and I can leave a small bottle for you there," she told the taxi driver. He asked her how much it cost and Celeste told him she'd be happy to give it to him, all she needed was his name, so she could tell Señor Mario.

"Regino García, at your service. You're most kind, señora."

When we arrived, I had to insist on paying the full fare, because the man didn't want to charge us. Celeste asked me which house was the Colonel's and I pointed at the ocher-colored construction halfway down the street.

"Well, let's go," the hyperactive character she'd suddenly become said. During the taxi ride I'd decided to tell her the full details of everything that had happened, because it was the only way she could help me put the five thousand pesos back in the Colonel's secretaire.

"I did something stupid," I said, and I told her about the loan I gave Güero, and I made her swear she wouldn't mention that name in front of my sister, because she knew him from when he was one of our employees in the furniture store. She placed her hand over her heart solemnly, and when I finished telling her everything about the situation, she asked me what she had to do. I let her in on my plan. I'd tell the Colonel that I came for my umbrella. Because I knew how cagey he was, he'd most likely tell us to wait. Then she'd ask permission to use his bathroom and the man wouldn't have any choice but to invite us in. Once we were inside his house, while she went to the bathroom, I'd manage to distract the Colonel and take him out to the patio with the excuse of asking him about his plants. She'd come out of the bathroom and put the money in the middle drawer of the secretaire, which was located near the entrance.

I gave her the five thousand pesos, which she put in her bag, and we walked over to ring the Colonel's bell. As I'd imagined, he didn't open the door with his pulley system, since he didn't know we were coming, and he shuffled down the passageway to open the door in person. We heard his steps approaching, and when he opened the door, even before he greeted me, he grabbed my umbrella, which he'd left beside the door, and handed it to me.

"I left it here knowing you'd come back for it," he said, and I stood there with the umbrella in my hand, looking stupid. But Celeste reacted expeditiously.

"I'm Celeste Hermenegildo, the nurse for Señor Eduardo's father. I wanted to ask you, please, if I might use your bathroom."

"Of course, I'll take you," the Colonel exclaimed, and, turning to me, added in his military manner: "Stay here and watch the entrance, don't let anyone in."

I stood there stiffly. The Colonel's order toppled our plan and I gave Celeste a panicked look, but she didn't flinch.

"Hold this, Eduardo, I won't be long," she said, handing me her bag where she'd just placed the five thousand pesos.

This is how things transpired. While the Colonel was leading the way, Celeste told him that she noticed that his neck looked somewhat stiff.

"You have a good eye," he said.

"Do you mind?" and she placed her hands on his upper back. They'd stopped in the middle of the passageway. "You have knots in this part, it's a shame I didn't bring my ointment with me."

"What ointment?"

They continued walking toward his apartment while Celeste explained that her ointment was excellent for rubbing out knots and back contractures.

"Do you think I have a contracture?"

"Let's take a look."

They went into the apartment and closed the door, leaving me on the street with my umbrella and Celeste's bag, and without any hope of returning his money.

But I hadn't counted on Celeste's presence of mind; she came out of the apartment and called, "Eduardo, please bring me my bag, I need my glasses. Señor Colonel says you should close the door, so no one sneaks in off the street."

I obeyed, closed the door, walked down the passageway, and went into the Colonel's house. Celeste took her glasses out of her bag and gave it back to me. She'd seated the Colonel on one of the chairs at the dining-room table, at an angle from which he could not see the secretaire.

"Let's see," she said to the Colonel, and moved closer to feel his neck.

"Didn't you have to go to the bathroom?" the master of the house asked.

"There's no rush, this won't take long."

"The one who needs to go is me, if you don't mind," I said to the Colonel, who granted me permission with a nod of his head.

Instead of going into the bathroom I went to the secretaire, removed the money from Celeste's bag, and opened the middle drawer. There was the bundle of photographs and under it the money bound with an elastic band. I grabbed the five thousand pesos and added them to the small bundle, then I closed the drawer and went into the bathroom, which was off to the side. I peed, flushed twice, and left. Celeste, still massaging the base of the Colonel's neck, turned to me and said, "I told Señor Colonel you can bring him a little bottle of ointment on Monday."

"It would be my pleasure," I said.

Including that one, there were now three little bottles I had to deliver: Mario's, the taxi driver's, and the Colonel's.

Celeste went to the bathroom, and when she came out, the Colonel, grateful for the massage, wanted to walk us to the door.

On the street, I waived a taxi down. Celeste's resourcefulness and poise astounded me. The slightly dull and introverted woman I knew at home had shown herself to be chatty and fearless on the street. Had it not been for her presence of mind, I'd have never returned Colonel Atarriaga's money. In the taxi I told her, "You saved me, Celeste," and I watched her without her noticing, trying to see her through my father's eyes, searching for something attractive. I didn't find anything, but my eyes were judging her, not my skin. She'd touched him countless times; her hands must have been the only thing he looked forward to when he woke up every day, and I wondered if she was aware of the immense power she held over him. Yes, she was; being outside the house with her showed me how profoundly aware of people she was; she knew Papá depended on her completely, to the degree that she could have killed him, in the event that his suffering got out of hand. With her experience, it would have been easy enough. Leave it to me, Señor Eduardo, I'll take care of it. It was as if I were listening to her say it, and I felt a sudden aversion to her limitless power.

I came out of my brooding when she touched my arm. We'd arrived. I paid the taxi driver and noticed that she was anxious. She rearranged her shawl and touched up her hair, as if she were going on a date. I pointed out the house where the Jiménez brothers lived. We knocked and the door was opened by the maid who, as usual, disappeared down the long hallway after we entered. For the first time both brothers were already in the living room, waiting for us, and I introduced them to Celeste.

"Celeste Hermenegildo, the nurse who takes care of my father."

She wasn't a nurse, but I felt obliged to conserve the status with which she'd presented herself to Colonel Atarriaga. I thought that Father Clark must

have let them know that I wouldn't be alone, because
the presence of Celeste didn't surprise them in the
least. Well, the remark only applies to Carlos Jiménez,
because the dimwit, as usual, hardly looked at us from
his wheelchair. His inexpressive face, illuminated by the
sun's morning glare, seemed like a cadaver's, and Celeste
clung to my side when we sat down on the sofa. Before
I opened my briefcase I looked at my watch to make it
clear that I came only to make up the twenty minutes
that I owed them from my previous reading session.
Carlos Jiménez also looked at his. Then, opening my
briefcase, I realized that I'd brought the wrong book;
instead of Capote's *In Cold Blood*, I'd brought my Isabel
Fraire book.

"Something wrong?" Carlos Jiménez asked.

"A mistake," I said, "I brought the wrong book."

"Whoa, that's bad!" the dimwit brother exclaimed.

Celeste grabbed my arm. The shrill voice of the
dimwit, should I say his fake voice, had frightened her.
I put my hand on hers to calm her and, addressing the
ventriloquist, I said as calmly as possible, "I see the
show's already underway."

"What show?"

It was obvious that he wanted to provoke me, scaring
Celeste, and I told myself that I'd made a mistake
bringing her along.

"What show?" the mute brother spit with his
mannequin voice, and Celeste flinched again.

"I'm scared," she said into my ear and squeezed my hand tightly.

Then, looking at the dimwit, I noticed that his face was smeared with some whitish cosmetic and he'd outlined his eyebrows with eyeliner to accentuate his dull appearance. They'd carefully made all the necessary preparations, it seemed, knowing I'd come with a woman.

Carlos Jiménez asked what book I'd brought instead of Capote's novel, and I told him it was a book of poems. He wanted to know whose, I told him, and he asked if Isabel Fraire was a good poet. I replied that yes, she was, and he ordered me to begin.

"Well, get started!" the mute shrieked.

Celeste lowered her eyes so she wouldn't have to look at him. She found something deeply disconcerting about that living cadaver. I opened the Isabel Fraire book and, clearing my throat, began to read: "Your skin, like sheets of sand and sheets of water swirling / your skin, with its louring mandolin brilliance / your skin, where my skin arrives as if coming home / and lights a silenced lamp—"

"Wait a minute!" Carlos Jiménez interrupted me. "Aren't you going to recite it?"

"That's what I'm doing," I said.

"From memory, I mean."

"I don't have it memorized. What's the difference?"

Carlos Jiménez turned to his brother. "Did you hear that, Luis? The young man with the beautiful voice intends to deceive us once again."

"He intends to deceive us once again!" his brother shrieked, eliciting another tremor in Celeste.

"When he reads a novel he has no idea what he's reading, and when he brings us a poem he doesn't know it by heart," Carlos Jiménez said.

I felt like getting up and smacking him.

"I'm not going to memorize this poem just to make you happy," I snapped.

Carlos Jiménez wore a sardonic smile.

"Did you hear that, Luis? The young man doesn't want to make us happy. Has he ever made us happy, Luis, despite his beautiful voice?"

"Never in a million years!" his brother answered.

Then something remarkable happened. Celeste, who'd kept her head lowered, began to murmur without looking up: "Your skin, like sheets of sand and sheets of water swirling / your skin, with its louring mandolin brilliance / your skin, where my skin arrives as if coming home / and lights a silenced lamp."

I stared at her, openmouthed.

"Go on," Carlos Jiménez told her, seeing that she'd stopped, and Celeste continued.

"Your skin, that nourishes my eyes / and wears my name like a new dress / your skin a mirror where my skin recognizes me / and my lost hand comes back from my childhood and reaches / this present moment and greets me / your skin, where at last / I am with myself."

She moved her head slightly to indicate that the poem had ended, and Carlos Jiménez turned to his brother. "Did you hear that, Luis?" and he applauded enthusiastically, mimicked by his brother.

"Of course, I heard!" the mute said. "The señora really knows what she's doing!"

Celeste bowed slightly to show her gratitude.

"I wonder if the señora knows another," Carlos Jiménez said.

"Yes, yes, recite another!" the moron shouted.

Celeste looked at me, as if asking for permission, and I nodded. She cleared her throat and began to recite the Isabel Fraire poem that begins "My life is wasted needlessly." The intensity of her voice was greater, and she delivered the words like my father, with a detachment that accentuated each word. I couldn't snap out of my astonishment. She'd memorized the poems he recited to her only by listening to them. I realized that she'd been in love with him all these years she'd lived with us. Maybe she still was, and I remembered she'd cried in the kitchen when she heard me reading my father's favorite poem, the one about skin, out loud. When she finished, the brothers applauded something fierce and the dimwit cried out in delight, this time with his own vocal cords. It was the first time I'd heard him emit one of his own sounds. Celeste, both smiling and afraid, squeezed my hand again.

Then Carlos Jiménez told his brother, "How clever our friend is, and he set up his little number so well! He brought this señora along and told us, just so he wouldn't have to read to us, that he brought the wrong book."

"Very clever!" the mute exclaimed.

"We have to acknowledge that he's not stupid at all, right Luis?"

"Not at all! There's nothing stupid about him!"

"And he accuses us of putting on a show! He set it up so well with this señoraza!"

"A señoraaaaaza!" the cripple screeched.

"Do you like the señora, Luis?"

"I loooove heeeerrrrrr!"

Celeste blushed beet-red. This time they were going too far. Carlos Jiménez shouted, "Señoraaaaaza!" and the moron repeated, "Señoraaaaaza!"

"Let's go, Eduardo!" she said, squeezing my hand.

Carlos Jiménez looked like he was about to stand up from his armchair: he braced himself on the armrests and began to tremble. His face was pierced by a look of disgust, as if someone had squeezed an entire lemon into his mouth, and then, to my astonishment, Luis, the mute, the moron, the sideshow puppet, put both his hands on the wheels of his chair, turned it in one fulminating motion, and told me, "Quick! Hold his head, he's having an attack!" and he wheeled himself forward toward the kitchen.

That sudden metamorphosis stunned me, and he, seeing that I hadn't moved, shouted, "For fuck's sake, my brother's having a seizure, do what I tell you!"

Carlos Jiménez had collapsed on the floor and shook from head to toe. Celeste, faster than me, knelt down next to him.

"Stick your hand in his mouth so he doesn't bite his tongue off!" Luis shouted from the kitchen. "Adela, quick!"

The servant appeared from the far end of the hallway and went into the kitchen without looking at us. Celeste opened Carlos's mouth with both hands and at that moment, a white foam gurgled out of it. Carlos Jiménez kept arching at a right angle and I thought he was going to snap in two. I'd knelt beside Celeste and asked her what I needed to do.

"Don't do anything," she told me.

Luis came out of the kitchen and reached us with three quick pushes on the wheels of his chair. I noticed how robust he was, despite his age. He had a tea towel on his lap, and on the tea towel a syringe. He picked up the syringe and ordered me to raise his brother's arm. I lifted Carlos Jiménez's arm and Luis pressed the needle in just below the shoulder. The liquid seeped in and when Luis removed the needle, his brother stopped heaving and relaxed on the rug.

"You can take your hand out of his mouth," Luis told Celeste, who did as she was told. Carlos Jiménez, when she removed her hand, looked at her with his mouth open and produced a whimper that sounded like a call for help.

"He's trying to tell me something," Celeste said.

"I doubt that he's going to tell you anything," Luis said. "He's mute."

PART TWO

I NEVER ASKED Margó Benítez about
her accident and I don't know if she ever
forgave me for that blunder. I should have,
but even though we used *tú* with each
other, I still felt like I was a home reader,
who has no business nosing around in the
life of his hosts. When I arrived at her
house there was a short bald man with
a sheaf of papers under his arm; he was
saying goodbye. The owner of the house
introduced him to me as her voice coach,
and I noticed that the papers were actually
musical scores. Margó introduced me
simply as "the young Eduardo" and Rómulo
Esparza regarded me with curiosity,

albeit with some aversion, like a man usually looks at a romantic rival.

"Margó has spoken about you at length," he said obsequiously and, flagrantly contradicting that phrase, he asked me what I did for a living. I told him that I was a home reader.

"How interesting. We are in the presence of an artist, then."

"No, not an artist at all, just a reader," I said, and Margó Benítez smiled, crowning me the victor in this sudden amorous duel that had just played out between me and the bald guy. Rómulo Esparza said goodbye to her and kissed her on the cheek, we gave each other an appropriate handshake, and Aurelia accompanied him to the door.

"He's an extraordinary pianist, and he also plays the guitar," the owner of the house told me, pointing to the armchair for me to sit, and she instructed Aurelia to bring the coffee. About the same time, I noticed the Daphne du Maurier novel on the side table and told her that I'd just finished reading it.

"Why?" she asked, surprised.

"I bought it in a used bookstore, and I read it from cover to cover that same night." And I added, seeing the disappointment on her face, "I wanted to know what the story was about; when I read here, I don't understand anything."

"So there's no point in reading any more of it since we've both already read the book."

She called Aurelia and told her to take the book away, which Aurelia did immediately. Her reaction left me speechless, because I thought she'd be happy that I'd read that book, which I told her.

"Happy? I was really hoping that the book would end up drawing you in," she said, "and now that's not possible, because you've already read it."

"It drew me in," I replied.

"Yes, but in your house, not here."

"I can't here, when I read out loud—"

"I know!" She interrupted me, wincing with annoyance. "It's my fault," she added somberly.

"What's your fault?"

"I was getting my hopes up that you were coming out of that bubble you live in, Eduardo, and that you'd start to read differently, like when you read me the poem the other day, but I was wrong. You'd rather read this book on your own, by yourself, and now I have nothing else to offer you."

"I read it because it's one of your favorite books and now it's also become one of my favorite books," I protested.

She shook her head, her eyes fixed on the rug, and said, "We were reading this book together and you just turned your back on me. It was simply a way to take a weight off your shoulders. Now that you've read it you've been exonerated from learning how to enjoy it with me. I didn't care that you didn't understand what you were reading; in the end you're a home reader and you can't be obliged to become engrossed by all the books you read."

"None of them engross me," I clarified so she wouldn't think it only happened with her.

"I was waiting for the moment," she continued, "when you were able to leave behind your home reader voice and you really began to experience what you were reading because it's my favorite book. I haven't stopped looking at you, waiting for that moment, and I've hardly paid any attention to the novel."

"You haven't been paying attention?"

"Not to one word, just like you. All I've done is watch you and listen to you."

I blushed intensely and tried to conceal it by raising the coffee cup to my lips without realizing that it was empty, which made her burst out laughing. At that moment Aurelia came in with the coffeepot, and maybe because of the relaxed atmosphere my awkwardness had facilitated, she leaned over more spectacularly than usual to fill our cups, producing an unexpected overflowing of boobs greater than all my expectations. Even Margó, in light of her maid's phenomenal glandular display, had a kind of retreat, as if ceding her the available space, and I wondered if it was something they'd rehearsed; as if Margó, unable to give me her body, was willing to offer me Aurelia's as a substitute. Aurelia returned to the kitchen and I raised the cup to my mouth, blowing on it to cool the coffee, a symbolic gesture to assuage the erection her spectacularly abundant bust had given me.

"You look so handsome in a sports coat," Margó told me.

She asked why I was dressed so elegantly and I told her I was going to the Reséndizes' house, that they liked me to dress a little more formally, because the last few times they'd taken it upon themselves to invite a few friends to my readings.

"Wow, look at you! What do you read them?"

"Poetry."

"And they understand it?"

"I don't know. I don't care."

"You don't care about anything."

She was smiling when she said it, but her words cut into me. I'd bought her favorite novel so I could read it and make up for my lack of emotional commitment in our reading sessions, and she, instead of being grateful, accused me of living in a bubble.

"Had I known you were going to get upset, I wouldn't have looked for your book and read it," I told her.

"Forgive me," she said quickly. "I'm not the easiest person to deal with."

There was a long silence, during which she continued to look at me. I took refuge behind my cup, and when I took a sip I burned my tongue. She noticed, laughed, and asked if I wanted a glass of water.

"No."

I looked in the direction of the kitchen, where I could hear Aurelia's voice, and her daughter's.

"You're doing everything you can to avoid looking at me," she said. "Do you feel sorry for an old paralyzed woman who's fallen in love with you?"

She said it in a way that was both gentle and mocking which, far from attenuating the bitterness of her words, accentuated it.

"You aren't old," I exclaimed, and I was about to add, And you're not paralyzed, either. It would have been stupid to say that, but somehow I realized that she was paralyzed only now that I heard it from her mouth, as if until that moment I would have believed that, simply by wanting to, she could get out of her wheelchair and start to walk.

In the sweetest voice I'd ever heard her use, she said, "How I've longed to tell you that!"

"That you're paralyzed?"

"No, that I love you!"

I looked in the direction of the kitchen, afraid that Aurelia had heard her.

"You keep criticizing me," I told her, lowering my voice, and I noticed that, speaking in such a way, I sounded like I was also in love.

"Because I love your remorseful expression," she said, still smiling. "Drink your coffee and go to the Reséndizes' house; today's rehearsal with Rómulo took a lot out of me. Give me the paperwork so I can sign it."

I took the visitation form out of my briefcase, she signed it, and when I shook her hand, she pulled me toward her and kissed me on the cheek. I felt her soft skin on mine and asked her, "Do you really think I don't care about anything?"

She looked at me soberly. "If you only knew how much I love you, Eduardo! Forgive me if I upset you," and she studied me with her dark eyes. We were about to kiss, hidden from Aurelia's view by the wall between us.

"Your skin is like cousin Raquel's," I told her.

"Don't tell me that. Raquel dies."

The thought struck me that such was the price of having skin like hers.

I DOUBT THE RESÉNDIZ COUPLE had been eagerly awaiting my arrival. The more or less small gathering the previous time had turned into an ultra-crowded soiree, and there were half a dozen of us reading poems tonight.

"Eduardo, how nice of you to come," Amalia Reséndiz exclaimed as she opened the door, and from those words I understood that I was just one more invited guest. Right there, at the door, she made me take off my tie. "Take off this boring outfit, they're going to mistake you for one of the waiters. You're an artist."

I had to give her my sports coat and she insisted that I untuck my shirt, emphasizing that it was really hot inside.

"I've invited a few other artists tonight, Eduardo. Come, I want to introduce you to my niece."

The house was packed with people, so the doors to the yard had been opened in order to gain additional space. There were in fact two waiters, although the guests were dressed informally, beginning with Amalia Reséndiz herself, who wore plaid slacks and a low-cut cotton blouse that gave the unpleasant impression that she was trying to look younger. Jeans and guayaberas were in abundance among the men. Many had gone into the yard because it was a warm evening, and as soon as I walked inside I saw Father Clark, who stood out because of his height, and he was the only guest who wore dark clothes. He was out in the yard accompanied by Ofelia; they each held a glass of wine and they chatted with a woman who had her back to me. Amalia Reséndiz had gone to look for her niece so she could introduce her to me; one of the waiters walked by with a tray of drinks and I stopped him to take a glass of white wine. I could still feel Margó's soft skin on my face where she'd kissed my cheek. Her reproaches, which in her house had seemed unfair, now, in the midst of that hubbub, accompanied me like a pleasant pronouncement of love, and I withdrew to a corner of the room with my glass of wine to savor them in plenitude, while pretending to observe the people around me.

Father Clark saw me, said something to Ofelia, and the three turned to look in my direction. We greeted each other from a distance, then Father Clark broke away from the two women and came inside to meet me.

"I am glad to see you, Eduardo," he said. "I was hoping to have a word with you." And pulling me aside, he added in a more confidential tone, "It is a good thing that you took matters into your own hands!"

"What matters?"

"This one," and he waved his arm in front of him, indicating the gathering we were part of.

"I have nothing to do with this, it was Amalia Reséndiz's idea."

"She told me you started these poetry soirees."

Ofelia came over, kissed me on the cheek, and introduced me to the woman who was with her, Deputy Director Ordóñez from the State Cultural Outreach Program.

"Congratulations are in order, Eduardo," the deputy director said. "Initiatives like this make all the difference."

I was going to ask her what difference she was referring to, and to what, when a woman who was behind her shouted her name; the deputy director turned around, in turn shouted her friend's name, and the two kissed each other with tremendous glee.

"I want to introduce you to Father Clark, something of an institution in our city," the deputy director said to the other woman, and Ofelia and I were momentarily forgotten.

"Let's move into the yard," I told her, "it's really hot in here."

She followed me, and circumventing the throng, we reached the coolest part of the property, where she asked me if it was true that I'd organized the gathering.

"Of course not, all of this was that crazy Amalia Reséndiz's idea. Had I known there were going to be so many people, I wouldn't have come."

I told her that the Reséndiz couple were the only ones who applauded when I finished each reading, and I was to blame for giving in to them, and now there's this artsy soiree.

"What's going on with these dress pants you're wearing?" she asked.

"Amalia took away my coat and tie at the door."

"You were wearing a coat and tie?"

"Yes."

"I don't believe you," and she started to laugh, discreetly at first and then harder, until she spilled a little wine from her glass. Two nearby couples looked at us. I forced myself to laugh so they'd think we were laughing at the same joke, and I realized how Amalia Reséndiz had manipulated me, first dressing me like a waiter and now undressing me so I wouldn't look like a waiter. Ofelia, continuing to laugh, shook her head and said, breathlessly, "My little brother in a coat and tie!"

"You made your point!" I rejoined, sulking.

"Settle down!" she said and the two couples turned to look at us again. Ofelia, annoyed, went into the house, leaving me alone, so I drank what was left in my glass to avoid their glances. I took out my cell phone, pretending I'd just received a message, fumbled with the little device, then put it away again. I missed Margó. The sensation of her soft skin on mine was still vivid, and I imagined that if she'd been beside me, we'd have laughed at that charade. I don't know what I'd have given to listen to her make fun of this pseudo-avant-garde evening in her surly, bedraggled voice. I kept reliving, over and over, the way she pulled me close so she could kiss my cheek and, mixed in with that amorous gesture, Aurelia's giant breasts appeared, which she took every opportunity to push in front of my face. Maybe I was falling in love with the older woman, stuck in her wheelchair, thanks to her maid's breasts, which were intended to compensate for her employer's disability, and I wondered again if Margó had instructed her to show them to me, subtly or not, any time she could, since Margó's condition prevented her from showing me her own body. I was suddenly overcome with an exuberance that made me look at the two couples and I bellowed, "Ladies and gentlemen," raising my empty glass in their direction. Margó loved me, even though I lived in a bubble, and Aurelia was the means to keep me at her side. Both couples raised their glasses, smiled at me, and once again ignored me, most likely thinking I was drunk. And I was, not from the alcohol but from feminine plenitude, from the possibility of being able to love in perfect carnal and spiritual harmony, not just one but two women.

"Here we've found the hermit!" a woman's voice called out behind me. It was Amalia Reséndiz, arm in arm with a beautiful young woman. She introduced me to Tatiana, her niece, who was holding my Isabel Fraire book in her hand.

"I took the liberty of opening your briefcase to take out your book, Eduardo, because I'd like to ask you a favor," the lady of the house said.

The favor consisted of me showing Tatiana a poem in the book so she could read it that evening. A love poem, preferably. I chose the one about skin because I'd memorized the page number.

"It's an extraordinary poem, Tatis, you'll be great," Amalia Reséndiz exclaimed. Tatis read it right there and, when she finished reading it, said that it was marvelous. "She's a poet who hasn't received the recognition she deserves," her aunt explained, repeating the exact words she'd heard me use on another occasion. Tatis asked where I'd bought the book. I told her, "In El Caracol," and I gave her the business card Abigael Martínez had given me, which I'd been using as a bookmark. I warned her that it was the last copy he had.

"Maybe they have another book of hers, other than this one," she said, and I thought maybe she wasn't as dumb as she looked. She took the card and asked if she could borrow my book for twenty minutes so she could memorize the poem. I told her she didn't have to memorize it, that she could just read it.

"No, poetry shouldn't be read, it must be felt," she declared with aplomb, and I thought she was as dumb as she looked.

She and her aunt went into the house, taking my book with them. I went into the house to look for Ofelia because I wanted to make amends, but I couldn't find her. Father Clark had also left.

Then Amalia Reséndiz beckoned everyone to be silent and asked those of us who were going to read to approach her. There were six of us, four men and two women, who closed ranks around our host. Tatis was missing; she was upstairs memorizing the skin poem.

The reading began, but it wasn't really that at all, because no one had anything in their hands, a definite sign that they were going to recite their poems from memory. I should've known, because for some people poetry and declamation are one and the same. What was I doing there?

A short, friendly-looking bald gentleman began, reciting from Neruda's *Twenty Love Poems and a Song of Despair*: "I can write the saddest lines tonight," et cetera. With a somewhat nasally voice, he dutifully disaggregated the poem and received a warm round of applause. In his wake was Señora Lucy, "who is going to delight us with three sonnets by the great poet Amado Nervo," Amalia

Reséndiz announced, and while Señora Lucy delighted
us I didn't take my eyes off the stairs, waiting for Tatis to
come down with my book. I was the last one in line to
read, so I was counting on having a little time before it
was my turn, but I was already sweating nervously. Señora
Lucy received a warm round of applause. Then it was the
turn of the señor who looked like a notary, whose name
Amalia Reséndiz called out but I've now forgotten, and
he delighted us with "Nocturne for Rosario" by Manuel
Acuña, and I remembered how my father made fun of
that poem when I was nearly a teenager. I was still drawn
to his unrestrained tackiness, especially the line that says
"Slice of my life." It seemed like a trap Acuña had set for
those reciting his poem, a kind of puddle in the path that
would trip them up, one from which the notary was also
unable to emerge unsoiled; until that moment he handled
it with a firm voice and a tone of heightened dignity but,
arriving at this point, he lost his bearings, took a deep
breath, and blurted out, as if in an act of protest, "Slice of
my life!" which sounded more like, "The house is on fire."
I lowered my eyes in embarrassment, though no one else
but me seemed to notice the mess, and the man received
the loudest applause to that point.

It was Señora Armendáriz's turn, who I literally did
not hear, because I was losing all hope that Tatis would
come down in time to hand over my book. I wasn't
certain she would in fact bring it down, because she
might have assumed that I, like everyone else, was going

to recite from deep inside my heaving chest. That said, the only poem I could have recited without reading it, because I'd already read it several times, was precisely the one she was memorizing. I didn't know any other poem and I started to go through it in my head while my neighbor, another bald gentleman, recited a fragment from the *Iliad*, in Greek, where Priam implores Achilles to return the dead body of his son Hector. His sobbing recitation earned him another warm round of applause, even though no one understood Greek.

It was my turn and Amalia Reséndiz called out my name. At that moment, I saw Tatis descending the stairs beside a young man whose arm encircled her waist, and I recognized him immediately. It was David, the guy who was always with Güero when he came to collect the monthly protection fee, the one who waited outside the furniture store. Both of them were laughing, but when his gaze met mine, he stopped smiling. As for me, I lost my concentration and made a mistake in the third line, which I repeated twice, and from there on I literally ran out of voice: I skipped lines six and seven and ended the poem with a murmur. I received an applause that was almost equally inaudible. Tatis Reséndiz took advantage of her place as the last to arrive and instead of standing beside us, she placed herself decidedly in front, directly in front of me, which I appreciated because she hid me from everyone's view. Although it was the same poem, I'm certain no one was able to connect my pitiful babble to her portentous declamation. Lifting both her arms, she uttered with a bellicose flourish: *Your skin, like sheets of sand and sheets of water swirling.* She paused and stood looking at those present. You could have heard a pin drop and then she returned to the charge to exclaim, *Your skin, with its louring mandolin brilliance,* pronouncing the word "louring" almost ferociously. She held us in her power, then abruptly lowered her voice in the following line and murmured, *your skin, where my skin arrives as if coming home,* to then shout like a banshee, *and lights a silenced lamp,* which again made us shudder. So that was her trick: move without rhyme or reason from a soft modulation to an irate one, without any connection to the meaning of the lines. It was clear that the poor woman hadn't understood a thing. Her voice, starving for effect, had made each line a separate thing, without any connection to the others. Like a lion tearing apart its prey.

The thunderous ovation she received made Amalia Reséndiz burst into tears.

TAKING ADVANTAGE of the commotion over Tatis's recital I went upstairs to look for my things, which I found on a chair in the foyer. I put the book, my tie, and my coat in my briefcase and I snuck out of the Reséndizes' house.

In the taxi that took me home my poor performance transformed before my eyes into a confrontational exploit. Destroying Isabel Fraire's poem had saved it from the declamatory success personified by Tatis. Lowering my voice until it was nearly inaudible had been an act of sabotage on my part.

But that reasoning fell apart when I went to bed. Beneath the sheets, alone, I once again experienced that sensation of failure. My performance had been pathetic. Fault of my arrogance, my vanity, I told myself, because from the beginning I'd felt superior to my recital colleagues, who now, as in the dark I reassessed their effort-filled performances, seemed almost admirable. They hadn't tried to do anything but delight the audience, with which they were in perfect harmony and the audience, like them, had a grandiloquent notion of what poetry is. Yes, they venerated the pompous verb, but their capacity to listen and their astonishment when they encountered the vibrancy of verse and rhyme were genuine. What right did I have to despise them?

I couldn't sleep and at times the idea that I'd acted like a guerrilla combatant reemerged and that my failure was honorable, but I immediately fell prey to another bout of bitterness. The most deplorable part was that I didn't care that I'd messed up in front of Amalia Reséndiz, who'd held me in such high esteem until now, or in front of her dunderhead niece, or in front of the official in charge of the State Cultural Outreach Program, just as I wouldn't have cared if Father Clark and Ofelia had been present for that meltdown; the only person before whose eyes it pained me to make a fool of myself was David the mobster, the one who stayed outside smoking when Güero paid us a visit to collect the envelope with our payment. I had the feeling that in his eyes my failure expanded until it reached the totality of my life and that this would give him the right from now on to blackmail me without regard.

The next day I felt seized by abstract rage. It had rained during the night, so I blamed it on that, and the sight of the wet yard brought back the objectivity I'd lost when I went to bed. The world looked fresh, and the recital from the night before seemed like a distant episode. I remembered the yard Isabel Fraire wrote about in one of her poems, a yard that intimidates its owners a little when they discover that it hardly needs their attention. I went to my room for the book, looked for the poem, and reread it. It ends with:

> Every three or four days
> > we say
> we have to buy seeds
> > fertilize the ground
> > irrigate
> > snip the dry flowers
> maybe we will
>
> meanwhile
> > the yard
> continues its own life   and we ours

That bittersweet ending, with that "maybe we will," left me submerged in a gentle gloom. That's how I'd been feeling lately, as if nothing in the world needed me, not my father, not the furniture store, not Ofelia, not my home reading program listeners. The world was a yard that was going to take care of itself, surviving without my attention, ignoring me like an attentive but superfluous spectator. I went back to the window to see if my yard was living its own life, and there, looking at the wet lawn and plants, I was overcome with a desire to do things, crucial and unequivocal things. In the meantime, remembering how the smile left David's face when he recognized me in the row of orators, I told myself that if I'd lost my concentration, he must have felt panic, knowing that I could tell his girlfriend's aunt the kind of activities the future husband of her niece was engaged in. I was, in short, a danger to him, and that was motive enough for him to decide to remove me from his extortion list.

Celeste had prepared the three little bottles of curative ointment her cousin Ramiro had delivered the previous afternoon, and I went to the bank to deliver Mario his and leave one for the taxi driver. I'd hoped to see Rosario and take her picture for my father. I arrived a few minutes after they opened, knowing I'd find her less busy then. I peeked into Mario's cubicle. He was alone, we shook hands, he asked me to sit down, and I gave him the ointment, explaining who the other bottle was for. He wrote the name Regino García on a little piece of paper.

"He might not even come by," I said.

"I'm always here. If he comes, he'll find me."

I heard Rosario's voice in the next cubicle; a one-and-a-half-meter-high wall separated us, and I thought she must have been with a client, or with one of the branch executives. She probably also heard my voice and thought I'd peek into her cubicle before long to say hello, which is what I usually did, but suddenly I didn't feel like seeing her, and I realized that what had happened a few days ago, when she made me wait for an hour outside the branch office without deigning to leave for one minute to have her picture taken for my father, enraged me. What would it have taken to send one of her underlings out to tell me she was unable to leave the bank? I raised the volume of my voice a little so that, knowing I was in Mario's cubicle, she'd come and apologize, but after five minutes nothing happened. Then, to prolong my visit, I asked about his tendonitis. He said that he didn't remember he had it most mornings but by the afternoon the pain started up again.

"How strong?"

"Strong enough, it climbs up to my elbow."

"Hmmm...that's not so good."

"No, not good at all."

"When you run out of the ointment let me know and I'll tell Celeste to get you some more."

"You're very kind."

"Not at all. And that elbow thing doesn't sound good either."

"No."

He looked at me with a sliver of impatience; he obviously had things to do and I wondered if he had a meeting with Rosario. I said no and stood up, he did the same, and we shook hands. To delay my departure from the bank and give Rosario yet another chance to come out and meet me, I searched for a large-peso banknote in my pants pocket and went to one of the cashiers to break it. I only had small bills. I had no other choice but to go to one of the open cashier windows and ask the bank teller to exchange a fifty-peso note for two-peso coins. I abhor having coins in my pockets, but I told myself that it's always a good idea to have a little change. Rosario didn't come out to greet me and I left the bank with twenty-five two-peso coins making a bothersome clamor in my right pocket, as well as having an ugly-looking bulge in my pants. In order to rid myself of that burden I decided to go to Sanborns de Piedra, where I arrived twenty minutes later. Gladis was taking a customer's order and, when she saw me, pointed to a table where she wanted me to sit. There was only one time that I disapproved of the table Gladis sent me to, because it was right in the middle of a draft of cold air. Sweetheart, she'd said when I complained, my whole area is full, look around, suck it up for a few minutes and once that little green onion who just asked for his check leaves, you can move to his table. I looked in the direction of the man she'd pointed out, a thin guy with a lumpy head that did actually look like a green onion, I sucked it up until he left and then I moved to his table.

She came to take my order with one of her favorite comments: "Are you leading the way for everyone else, little boy? Where are the rest of your kindergarten classmates?"

I told her they were coming, and that I had a craving for some huevos rancheros. She recommended some Gerber baby food, pear, which was quite tasty.

"I'm tired of that pear mush," I told her. "Rancheros would be better."

She wrote my order down in her pad: rancheros, café Americano, and grapefruit juice. She removed the extra place mats from my table and said, "Mireya told me you were flirting with her the other day."

"Damn it! She promised she wasn't going to tell you."

"I killed her. Does that bother you?"

"You did the right thing; the rolls she served me were flat."

"That's what they told me, that's why I killed her." She saw something was wrong, because she added: "Nene's got something on his mind. A lover's quarrel?"

"Maybe," I told her, giving her the menu and she left to turn in my order. I dialed Ofelia's number, but she didn't answer. I assumed that she didn't want to speak to me. Gladis came back with my huevos rancheros ten minutes later.

"Talk to your mami," she said, and it occurred to me that in a city where half the population lived closed up in houses and yards surrounded by high walls, it was really only possible to open up to a waitress from Sanborns.

"She's your age," I said.

"Twenty-two?"

"Give or take a year."

Between bites I told her about Margó, leaving for the very end that she was paralyzed.

"Are you joking?"

"No, I'm serious. From the waist down. She uses a wheelchair."

I didn't have to guess what she was thinking; her question was enough.

"Paralyzed all over, Nene?"

"I think so."

She sighed like a mother observing her child take up a profession beneath his capabilities.

"You're going to need plenty of endurance."

I didn't say anything and she left to take another customer's order.

The strange thing about talking to waitresses at Sanborns is that they walk away and come back, not pausing for a minute, and the conversation moves forward in fits and starts. There's no need to lose hope, that perpetual movement endows their remarks with overwhelming wisdom, which makes them extremely valuable when one requires guidance of any kind. It took me a while to catch on to that peculiar dialectic, but now I'd mastered it and I couldn't imagine chatting with Gladis, with Luz Aurora, or with Tristana while seated comfortably in an armchair, where they would have most certainly lost their wisdom.

My cell phone rang. It was Ofelia. She asked where I was and I told her. "I acted like a real asshole yesterday," I added.

"That sounds about right."

"I looked for you after, but you weren't there, and neither was Father Clark."

"We left because of the crowd and the heat."

"You looked like a couple."

"I'll let you know when we are," and she asked how my reading had gone. I told her it was shitty and that I'd tell her about it later. We hung up, both pacified.

Fighting with Ofelia drove me crazy. Gladis came back five minutes later, when I'd finished the rancheros; she took my plate and asked if I wanted anything else. I told her I didn't, and she asked, "Why do you like women who are older than me, Nene?"

"It's just that my mother had enormous breasts, which left me traumatized."

"You're a jackass," she exclaimed. "What are you talking about, huge breasts! I remember her, her breasts were beautiful. She was the most elegant woman in all the Sanborns."

I looked at her fondly. Gladis told you where to sit, and she could tell you things you didn't know about your mother.

"She had enviable skin," she added, and her words made my heart race.

"Are you serious?"

"Like a princess," she said. "Children don't notice these things."

"What does skin like a princess look like?"

"It's the kind that's so thin you can see the little veins. A complexion so pure it would make a king fall in love with her."

Gladis hadn't even finished grade school and she was still so damn articulate.

"She must've smelled good, too," I said, enthralled.

She laughed without taking her eyes off me, more cunning than a fox. "Sure, Nene," she said. "Just like your princess, I'm sure." She took the bill out of her skirt pocket and placed it on the table. I'd started to blush. "You want more coffee?"

I said I didn't. She walked away and I sat there absorbed in the news that my mother had privileged skin, something no one had ever told me and I'd never noticed. Gladis was right, children don't notice their mother's skin, which completely covers her, and only when they grow up and fall in love, when they give and receive their first kisses, the skin they love seems like a separate thing to them, and then they learn to say "Your skin," like Isabel Fraire does in her poem.

I DIDN'T FEEL like going to the furniture store, so I started walking aimlessly. I was still seized by some abstract rage. Ten minutes later my cell phone rang and an unknown number appeared on the screen. It was Tatis Reséndiz. She was in El Caracol and wanted to know the name of the poet who wrote my book, because she'd forgotten it.

"Isabel Fraire," I answered. She thanked me and I asked who'd given her my number.

"My aunt."

I thought that was odd. None of the owners of the houses where I did my readings knew my number. It was a program rule that everything had to be mediated by Father Clark.

"Congratulations on last night," I told her.

She thanked me. I waited for her to say something, but she was quiet. I had a hunch she was with David. Maybe he was the one who'd given her my number, not her aunt. If that was the case, she was aware of the fact that we knew each other, and I wondered if she knew that her future husband was engaged in the extortion business.

"Well, thanks again, I have to go," Tatis said, and she hung up.

My good mood had gone to hell. If Tatis knew what her boyfriend did, I didn't pose any threat to David and my power over him was nonexistent, and maybe not only Tatis but Señor and Doña Reséndiz themselves were aware of everything, and they pretended they didn't know. What, after all, did I know about them, beyond the fact that they were fatuous and loved to be surrounded by other people?

I kept walking. I'd distanced myself from all my friends after the misfortune, as Celeste called it, and since my friends were protected inside walled-in gardens, I'd distanced myself from gardens. Now that I couldn't drive I walked through the city, noticing all the walls in the City of Eternal Spring, which was abundant with streets that were no more than open-air tunnels lined with vertical brick walls made out of cinder block or volcanic stone, *piedra*. So much wall had infected the people: housekeepers, business owners, and taxi drivers, the beautiful woman from the Vista Hermosa neighborhood, too; everyone walked around stone-faced. There was even a Sanborns made out of stone!

Half an hour later, tired of rambling aimlessly through so much erected stone, I went to the furniture store to see if grim-faced Jaime needed anything.

When I entered the store I found a book of poems by Gianni Rodari on one of the tartan sofas. Jaime told me that a woman who'd just bought a desk with a hutch for her son's room had left it behind. It had probably fallen out of her bag when she sat on the sofa to try it out. I vaguely remembered the name Rodari, knew he was an internationally acclaimed Italian writer of children's books, and out of curiosity, I opened the book at random and read a poem. I liked it so much that I sat on the tartan sofa so I could continue reading, despite Jaime's reproachful look; he would have never allowed himself to sit on a chair or sofa we wanted to sell. I remembered what my father told me and Ofelia when he came across an anodyne poem: It's missing the three *p*'s: purpose, prowess, and prudence. Rodari's poem reverberated purpose, prowess, and prudence, as well as an intense melancholy. I read two more poems, and I took the book home with me. That same afternoon I read the poems in the Vigil family house, never imagining the consequences this would have. Rodari's poems *sounded*, their ludic and outlandish rhymes could be heard outside the domain of my lips, which had until that moment been the only organ in that house used to decipher the written word.

> One day, on the Soria express train to Monteverde,
> I watched a man come aboard; his ear was green—
>   verde.
>
> He was no longer young, but seasoned, it seemed,
> everything but his ear, which was completely green.

The three boys couldn't resist its music, though at first
I didn't notice it, and perhaps I only noticed that their
eyes didn't possess that hypnotic fixity their parents' and
grandmother's had, which came from fixating on the
mouth of the one speaking.

> *So I could see him better, I changed my seat*
> *to study the marvel, to get a better look at least.*
>
> *I asked: Señor, please tell me, you are of a certain*
>   *age,*
> *that green ear of yours, does it serve you some*
>   *advantage?*
>
> *You can call me old, he said and winked, I've lived*
>   *my years,*
> *but from my younger days all I've kept is this ear.*

I'd decided to read them Rodari's poems without any
clear intention, other than the pure excitement reading
them gave me, but when I saw that the three little boys
were *listening* to me for the first time, I wanted to make
sure that they were really listening to me with their ears,
not with their eyes, to this end I raised the book just
enough so it was in front of my mouth, and I continued
reading. The father, the mother, and the grandmother
stretched their necks so they wouldn't lose sight of my
lips, but the boys didn't move at all. I stood up, turned

around, turning my back on the whole family, and I
continued reading out loud:

> *It's a child's ear, which helps me heed*
> *things adults don't stop to feel*
>
> *I hear what trees say, the birds that sing,*
> *the stones, rivers, and the clouds passing,*
>
> *I also hear the children, the ones spinning fables*
> *that an older ear hears most incomprehensible.*

The father stood up and asked me what I was doing. I
didn't answer him and kept reading:

> *The green-eared man spoke just like this*
> *that day on the Soria to Monteverde express.*

"Turn around, we can't see you!" he ordered. He was
beside himself. "Why are you turning your back on us?"

"Because I have a booger in my nose," I replied, still
with my back turned, and the boys roared with laughter.

Their father turned to them, furious. "Why are you
laughing? What did he say?"

The oldest one responded timidly, "That he has a
booger in his nose."

"Why are you hearing him?"

"Because he's funny," the youngest one replied.

"What's so funny?"

"What he's reading."

"You don't have to hear him," the father shouted.

I closed the book with a sharp thud, opened my bag, and, while I placed the book inside it, I turned toward the three adults, making sure they could see my mouth perfectly.

"I'm leaving this house and you'll never see me again," I said, my voice trembling. "Forcing your children to be deaf! You can't hear the rhyme, but they can!"

I closed my briefcase with a quick slap and I took a step toward the door. The mother shot up like a coil spring.

"Wait, don't go."

Her husband took her by the arm, but she jerked it away and said in a beseeching voice, "Please, sit down and continue reading."

"The poems?"

"Yes."

The father looked at the mother but she ignored him. I went back to my chair, opened my briefcase, and took out the book in the middle of a silence even a deaf person could have heard. The mother sat back down. The father, who was still standing, seeing that I was looking at him, waiting to resume the reading, had no other choice but to sit down as well. A revolution had just occurred in that house: The boys had permission to *hear*.

———

Two days later, back in the furniture store, I
received a call from Abigael Martínez. I thought he must
have found another copy of Isabel Fraire's collection
of poems and wanted me to return the one that had
been inscribed for him, but that wasn't why he called;
instead, he wanted to tell me that a few days ago a young
woman had come into his bookstore, accompanied by
her boyfriend, asking if he had any book by Isabel Fraire,
and he wanted to know if I'd sent them. I told him I had.

"I suspected as much," he said. "Turns out that
today the boyfriend came back, accompanied by another
fellow, and he demanded that I pay eight thousand pesos
a month for a protection fee."

"Eight thousand?"

"Yes."

I asked him what the man with David looked like
and, from the description he gave me, I came to the
conclusion that it was Güero.

"Are they friends of yours?" Abigael Martínez asked
me.

"Are you asking if I'm also in the extortion business?"

"No, but you sent them."

"I sent the girl," I told him, "because she was looking
for a book by Isabel Fraire and she's the niece of some
acquaintances of mine."

"Amalia Reséndiz?"

"Yes."

"That lady called me the next day to suggest that
I host an evening event of music and poetry in my
bookstore, a soiree she called it, in honor of Isabel Fraire.
I asked her who would cover the expenses for this soiree,
and she told me that I would, if I'd be so kind, and the
soiree would give citywide visibility to my bookstore."

"What did you say to her?"

"That the business is just getting on its feet
and I can't spend what little money I have on wine,
sandwiches, and chair rentals. The lady got upset and
almost hung up on me. The guy who blackmailed me
a few hours ago demanded that I not only pay the
protection fee but that I also organize the poetry soiree
within the next eight days, otherwise things will get
really ugly."

This was how I learned that Amalia Reséndiz was
avaricious, and I guessed that David, when he saw that
his future aunt-in-law was angry, decided to strong-arm
Abigael. I was in part responsible for what had happened,
because if I hadn't mentioned the name of the bookstore
to Tatis, Abigael wouldn't have received a visit from
her thug of a boyfriend, nor would he have received a
call from Amalia Reséndiz, and now, at least for a little
while, he'd still be moving through the labyrinth of his
books worry-free.

"Listen," I told him, "the guy who's shaking you down
is the fiancé of the girl and he's doing the same to me."

"How much is he charging you?"

"The same as you."

That wasn't true; they charged me two thousand pesos less. Either the conditions of the situation had gotten worse or Güero had actually managed to obtain preferential treatment for us.

"I didn't know things worked like this," he said. "I've never run my own business before."

His voice sounded less anxious now that he knew we were in the same boat.

"I don't think the girl or her family know how this guy makes his living," I told him. "If I let them in on his secret, he's capable of killing me or setting fire to the furniture store. And Amalia Reséndiz is an impetuous woman; once she gets an idea in her head, no one can change her mind. She wants to have this soiree so her niece can swagger around reciting poetry. There was a recital in her house three nights ago; her niece destroyed one of Isabel Fraire's poems, but all eyes were on her. I'm sure she wants to do the same thing again, but this time with a larger audience."

Abigael remained silent and the silence lasted so long that I thought he must have been crying. I had the urge to loan him some money to help meet the costs of the poetry soiree, but I stopped myself. My economic situation wouldn't allow it: The furniture store was going from bad to worse and the despair I heard in Abigael's voice forced me to admit that his situation wasn't any different from mine, just that I was used to it. Keeping a business going in this city, with people's purchasing power at rock bottom, and the protection fees on top of that, was a little less than miraculous. In the face of such general impoverishment my only hope was that the criminals themselves would eventually go away.

"Have you been to Sanborns de Piedra?" I asked Abigael.

"Yes," he replied.

"I'll buy you breakfast tomorrow morning."

He was quiet, and then he said, "Thanks, but not there. I got mugged there once."

"In Sanborns de Piedra?"

"Yes."

"When?"

"Last year."

"In the restaurant?"

"No, in the tobacco section of the store. They took my money at gunpoint, but they were discreet about it, then they left."

My jaw practically hit the floor. Why hadn't Gladis mentioned anything? There was no way she didn't know. Maybe they'd been instructed to keep their mouths shut so the establishment wouldn't look bad? It was my second home, Gladis and Tristana had watched me grow up, Papá would take us there for breakfast religiously every Sunday morning, and I realized I had an unshakable conviction that nothing bad could happen in that place.

So, to my regret, we went to the Sanborns Father Clark frequented, where they served flat rolls. We met at eight because Abigael opened the bookstore at ten, and we arrived within a minute of each other. I ordered rolls and coffee and put a lot of emphasis on wanting my rolls fluffy, not flattened out. Abigael went for something safer and ordered the Swiss enchiladas and a glass of the seven-fruit juice. They brought me flat rolls, but I didn't complain; on the contrary, I was pleased to confirm that they didn't know how to make them any other way in that place.

Suddenly, while we were eating, Abigael put his fork on his plate, looked around, and confessed that he'd been mistaken; he'd been mugged in this Sanborns, not in the Piedra one. I didn't say anything, but it infuriated me that he was so wholly unapologetic about it; I was eating these horrible flat rolls because of his awful memory.

"All the Sanborns are the same," he said to justify his confusion, and that's when I pounced.

"That's not true at all! This one is nothing like the Piedra one."

"I don't see any difference," he snapped.

We looked at each other, a current of mutual disdain crossed what little space there was between us. I placed my fork on my plate to give my words greater emphasis. "Apart from the rolls, on which, modesty aside, I consider myself an expert, the coffee they serve in the other one is much better than this."

"It's the same coffee!"

"It's the same coffee, but they reheat it here, there they don't."

That wasn't true; they reheated it in both places, but I was determined to show Abigael that not all Sanborns are the same. In what other Sanborns would I find waitresses as intelligent and mischievous as Gladis and Tristana?

Animosities can sprout out of the most trivial discussions, like the one I was having with Abigael about whether one Sanborns could be better than another. I wondered why I'd invited him out for breakfast to begin with, and I found the answer right away: because of my long-running habit of feeling responsible for the misfortune of others. But now, seeing how he was devouring his Swiss enchiladas, accompanied by a large glass of seven-fruit juice, the most expensive drink on the menu, he didn't seem so wretched, and my compassion toward him was giving way to antipathy. I told myself I couldn't be blamed for David charging him a fee so he could be left to work in peace. It was like that for all of us, and his bookstore wasn't going to be an exception. Regarding the poetry soiree they were making him organize, who could be sure it wasn't going to help out the bookstore? There was some truth in the fact that the event would give some publicity to his little shop.

He raised his hand to get the attention of the waitress and ordered a double cappuccino. My rancor intensified as I looked at the generous provision of liquids with which he was regaling himself at my expense: café Americano, a double cappuccino, and a glass of seven-fruit juice. Now all he had to do was order a beer at nine in the morning. He looked at my miserable flat rolls and asked, "Aren't you going to order anything else?"

"I'm fine with this."

At some point, in the middle of our muddy dispute about the best Sanborns in the city, we had started to use *tú* with each other. Something he'd told me about Isabel Fraire had continued to bother me and I asked him if he knew who the individual was that Isabel Fraire sometimes came to see.

"Why's it matter?"

"I'm curious."

He'd finished his enchiladas and juice; he took a sip of his coffee and cleaned his lips with his napkin. His green eyes offset his ugly mouth, thin and wide like the opening in a piggy bank, and I wondered if he was the mysterious person. However, one doesn't get rid of a book inscribed to you by the woman who was your lover. He cleared his throat and repeated what he'd already told me: He didn't know the identity of the man Isabel came to see in our city, but he suspected that his wife knew more about it, because the two had been very close. However, his wife had died without telling him anything about it. That's how I found out that Abigael Martínez had been widowed two years before, but I nodded with a contrite air to prevent the conversation from being diverted to his late wife, and told him, "Maybe the man Isabel saw was a writer like her."

"No, he wasn't a writer or artist."

"How do you know?"

"It's a hunch. I think he was one of those perfect family men, an average guy, probably even had gray hair. Isabel had a soft spot for that sort of person."

My heart beat faster and I tried to remember when my father started to talk so enthusiastically to us about Isabel Fraire's poems. It was hard to know. I had the impression that her name had always been spoken in our house. Maybe she and my father had met inadvertently, and I asked Abigael if Isabel Fraire had ever given a reading in our city.

"No, absolutely not. She always said this city has no soul, only swimming pools."

"Wait. Say that again, please," I cried out, sitting forward in my seat.

"What?"

"What you just said, what Isabel Fraire used to say about this city."

"She said that it has no soul, only swimming pools. Why?"

"That's something my father always says. I've heard him say it hundreds of times."

He noticed my agitation and he paused midmotion as he raised the cup to his lips. "Well, maybe it's something people say around here."

I shook my head. "If he'd heard someone else say it, he would have said, 'As the saying goes, this city has no soul, only swimming pools.' I know him."

He took a sip of coffee and sat back, hitting the back of his chair. "You mean to say that Isabel and your father knew each other?"

"I think so."

He leaned forward again and added, "You mean to say that your father is the man Isabel Fraire would meet when she came here?"

PART THREE

WHEN SHE OPENED the door, Aurelia
was talking on the phone with her
employer, she had the cordless phone next
to her ear, and she told Margó Benítez
that I'd just arrived. She was wearing a
copiously low-cut linen dress and it was
impossible not to look at her dark breasts
that contrasted with the garment's white
fabric. She motioned for me to come into
the house and close the door behind me,
which I did, and I sat in my usual seat
while she continued talking. Yes, señora,
of course, we'll talk tomorrow, she said
to the phone, and when I thought she
was going to hang up, she exclaimed, Are

you okay, sweetheart? and I realized she was talking to her daughter. So, we were alone. She exchanged a few more words with her daughter and then hung up. She then explained that Señorita Margó was in Valle de Bravo, where one of her sisters lived, and she'd taken Griselda, her daughter, with her, and she apologized for not telling me beforehand. I was surprised that Margó, knowing that I'd just arrived, hadn't wanted to speak to me directly to apologize herself. Aurelia offered me a cup of coffee, because that's what her employer had just instructed her to do, and I sensed that I could have told her to do anything, as if it were her duty to be at my service in recompense for the absence of the owner of the house. I accepted the coffee; she went to the kitchen and shortly after returned and said, "We've run out of coffee. Want some tequila?"

I said I did and I was surprised that instead of taking a bottle from the liquor cart, she disappeared down the hallway, from which she returned almost immediately carrying a bottle of tequila and wearing her usual wide-mouthed smile. I noticed that it was a cheap brand. She took a tequila glass out of the buffet hutch, filled it, and gave it to me.

"You aren't going to join me?" I asked her and, without waiting for her to respond, I told her I could drink coffee by myself but not tequila.

"Okay, but only a little nip, Señor Eduardo."

It was the first time she'd pronounced my name.

She removed another glass from the hutch and served herself. She swallowed half the contents in one gulp, and I realized that she was used to drinking. I assumed the tequila was her own and that this gave her the freedom to pour us as much as we wanted.

"Why don't you sit down?"

"No, I'm fine like this," she said.

I drank my tequila in two gulps, and she leaned over to fill my glass again.

"Very tasty," I told her. "Are you sure you don't want to sit down?"

"No."

It was clear that she didn't think it was appropriate to sit and have a drink with me, but seeing her there, on her feet, made me uncomfortable, and I wondered if she might not be a little off in the head, the way she was always smiling. I drank my second glass in two gulps, leaned my head against the back of the armchair, and closed my eyes, pretending I was tired. I don't know what I wanted to show her by doing so. Maybe I was hoping that, if she saw I was relaxed, she'd feel like sitting down, or maybe I was just really tired, and two tequilas in a row had suddenly loosened me up.

"Would you like to lie down, Señor Eduardo?" she asked me.

"Where?" I asked her.

"In my room, or in Señorita Margó's. Lie down for a bit and you'll feel better."

"I feel fine, I'm just tired. Did you put something in my tequila?"

"Of course not," she answered.

"I'm only joking," I said.

"Stand up, I'll take you to Señorita Margó's room."

The truth was that I did feel tired.

"Only ten minutes," I told her.

"Yes, have a little nap, then I'll wake you."

I stood up and followed her down the hallway. We entered a spacious, well-lit room where a wheelchair sat beside the window. She told me to take off my shoes and lie down and then she closed the curtains to darken the room. I took off my shoes, I lay down, faceup, and it suddenly occurred to me that all of this was some kind of ruse arranged beforehand, I don't know if by Aurelia or by Margó herself.

"I'll wake you in a little bit," she told me with her unfailing smile.

"I'm not tired."

"It doesn't matter, rest for a bit." She left the room and closed the door.

I closed my eyes and little by little fell asleep. When I woke it was dark outside and the small lamp on the bedside table illuminated the room with its faint light. Aurelia, apparently, had entered at some point to turn it on so I, when I woke, wouldn't find myself immersed in absolute darkness. I sat up and looked for my shoes, which were right beside my feet. On the bedside table

there was a picture frame with a photograph of Margó.
It had been taken before the accident. She was standing,
wearing a bathing suit, on the seashore and looking away
from the camera. She was taller than I'd imagined and
her pose, how she turned to the side, highlighted the
thickness of her thighs, which were long and enticing.
As I'd suspected, hers was not a body made with a single
stroke. She gave the impression of a woman pieced
together, who was on the verge of decaying into parts.
Her dominant thighs, her profile, the seashore, and her
disheveled hair gave her a voluptuously inconclusive
aura, almost savage, and it occurred to me that this
extraordinary photograph had been placed there so I'd
see it when I woke.

I put on my shoes, and when I stood up, I felt vaguely
dizzy. I walked to the door and opened it. The house
was quiet and dark. I went back down the hallway to
the kitchen. Aurelia wasn't there, and she wasn't in the
living room. I went back to the hallway, knocked on the
first door; there was no answer, so I opened it. It took a
few seconds for my eyes to adjust to the dark. Aurelia
was lying on a bed, facedown and naked, and one of her
legs, bent at an angle, made her ass bulge. I moved closer
and said her name, but she only snored in response.
It occurred to me that knowing she was ugly, she'd
decided to get drunk so I'd surprise her like this, asleep
and naked, trusting that this would be the best way to
enflame my desire. In fact, it was, because seeing her in

that posture within hand's reach, snoring softly, turned me on, and I shook her so she'd wake up and we could make love. But she didn't respond. If this had been her strategy to seduce me, the fool had gone too far.

I sat on the edge of the bed, waiting for her to come to, and I wondered if perhaps she'd lied to me about the telephone, making me believe that her employer and daughter were in Valle de Bravo so I'd feel emboldened to seduce her. If the phone call had been a ruse, Margó might show up at any moment, and finding me in her house at this hour with Aurelia stripped naked in her bedroom, she might think that I got her drunk so I could take advantage of her, so I left the room without making a sound, searched in the dark living room for my briefcase, and fled like a thief in the night.

When I got home, I went straight to my room. Celeste and my father had already gone to bed. I undressed, got into bed, and turned out the light. But I wasn't tired, and while I thought about Margó's voluptuous thighs, about her body, mysteriously made of parts more assembled than pieced together, and her formidable legs that, because they lacked sensitivity and movement, were now somehow more imposing, I asked myself again whether that photograph had been placed there so I'd fall in love with that body, obviating her present misery with the knowledge of her past splendor.

———

I WENT TO COLONEL ATARRIAGA's house in
the afternoon to give him Celeste's ointment. When I
knocked, he pulled the cord to let me in; I traversed the
long passageway and pushed open the door to his house,
which he'd left ajar. That part surprised me, because he
always met me at the door wearing that grim expression
of his. He was in the living room, sitting in his armchair,
and I noticed he was wearing a different robe and other
house slippers, which seemed to be new. His appearance
also seemed different: He'd combed his hair and I
noticed a scent of lavender.

"Should I close it?" I asked him.

He winced and asked where Celeste was. I told him
she was at my house and added that I brought him the
ointment for his sore muscles. I opened my briefcase, took
out the little bottle, and gave it to him, but he didn't take it.

"She told me she'd be coming," he said brusquely. He
kept me standing, the little bottle still in my hand, and I
couldn't bring myself to sit down.

"I don't remember her saying that, Colonel," I said as
gently as I could.

"You were in the bathroom, Señor... Señor...!
What's your name?"

"Eduardo."

"You were in the bathroom! She told me she'd come
back today to massage my neck."

He was outraged, his hands grasping the arms of
his chair. I assumed that while I put the money back

into the drawer of his secretaire, Celeste, to keep him
calm, told him that she'd return next time to give him
a massage and, now that the danger had passed, she'd
forgotten her promise.

"I'm sorry," I told him.

"Easy for you to say!" he exclaimed. "Here I am
waiting for her, and you're sorry. Call her and tell her to
get over here, that I'm waiting for her!"

"I can't do that; she can't leave my father alone."

"Go take care of your father yourself!"

It might have been the first time that I really looked
at him. It might also have been the first time that he
really looked at me.

"You have no right to tell me what I have to do," I told
him.

It took a while for my sentence to sink in, or maybe
it's a military technique to not respond at once to a
subordinate's disobedient act, so the latter perceives,
through the silence of his superior, the enormity of his
action and punishes himself before the other does so.
Finally, he said, "You are expiating a crime. I shouldn't
have allowed you into my house. How dare you talk to
me like that? Get the hell out of here."

"I'm leaving, but you'll have to sign the visitation
form first," and I opened my briefcase to take out the
paperwork. I was standing in an uncomfortable position,
and when I opened it the Rodari book, *The Tartar
Steppe*, and a few invoices from the furniture store fell to

the floor, among them the picture of the Colonel in the arms of a younger woman, which I'd forgotten to return to his secretaire.

The invoices and picture landed at his feet, the latter caught the Colonel's eye and he placed his house-slippered foot on top of it, leaned over to pick it up, looked at it, looked up, and asked me, "What's this photograph doing in your briefcase?"

I didn't say anything, and he didn't wait for me to respond; he stood up and went to the secretaire while I knelt down to pick up what had fallen on the floor. I put everything away and closed my briefcase. The Colonel was counting the money that was in the drawer. When he finished, he put the stack of bills in the pocket of his robe, turned around, looked at me, and said in a voice breaking with emotion, "I didn't have so many five-hundred-peso bills. You got into my money the day Celeste came with you."

"I didn't steal anything from you," I said, "you just saw that, and I can explain what happened."

"I don't know what you did, but you got into my money. I don't want to hear any explanation."

"I'm not a thief," I told him.

"Get out," he said, opening the door.

"I'm not a thief," I repeated.

"I said get out."

I left his house and walked down the long passageway leading to the street, opened the door, and the Colonel pulled hard on the cord, whipping the door closed with a bang behind me.

At home, when Papá dozed off in front of the TV, I told Celeste what had happened. She remained unperturbed as she listened to me and then said, softly so she wouldn't wake my father, "I don't think he'll call the police."

"Why not?"

"He hates the police; he told me while you were in the bathroom, Eduardo."

"He hates me more."

"Do you want me to go see him?"

"What are you going to tell him?"

"I'll think of something."

There she was again, the Celeste I didn't know, determined and fearless. She called her niece and asked her to come early the next day to take care of my father. I took Papá to his room in his wheelchair and she helped me stand him up. While I supported him, she held the plastic urinal so he could pee for the last time of the day. I couldn't avoid seeing his penis and I looked away. But not Celeste, who made sure he didn't piddle outside the basin, and then she absorbed the last drops on his penis with toilet paper and pulled up his underwear. Between the two of us we put him to bed.

It was late so she went to bed, too. I read a while, turned out the lights, and also went to bed. At two in the morning I woke to the sound of my father moaning;

I was going to get up when I heard Celeste's footsteps in the hallway, then I heard them speaking. I stayed awake for a while and then fell back asleep, but that didn't last long. I got out of bed and went to the kitchen for a glass of water. I could hear the sound of my father snoring from the hallway. Then I stopped. My father didn't snore like that. I retraced my steps and nudged the door a little, which was already slightly open. I recognized Celeste's silhouette lying next to my father. Her back was to him, and he embraced her from behind. A timid embrace, as if he didn't want to disturb her. I closed the door and went back to my room, forgetting about the glass of water.

I tossed and turned in my bed, but I couldn't sleep. The way my father was embracing Celeste, clutching her back while she snored, gave me a feeling of profound and hopeless exclusion. I was getting in the way. More than anything, her snoring gave a certain I don't know what kind of degradation to my future in that house, as if I were an intruder eavesdropping on other people's lives. I thought that Celeste and I shared that complicity which is so natural between the healthy who care for the ill. Now I realized that the real collusion was between the two of them behind my back. The real sick person in the house, after the accident (or the misfortune, as Celeste called it), was me, almost thirty-five years old and living like a kept man, because ever since they'd taken away my license we had to pay a guy to deliver the furniture store orders with our truck, which had been my principal function up to that point. My only contribution to the family business had been reduced to going over the accounts with Jaime, and I hadn't even been able to call the futon lady, closing a practically certain sale.

The next day I woke to the voices of Celeste and Clotilde, her niece, who'd arrived early to take care of my father. By the time I went to the kitchen for breakfast, Celeste had already left. I took a shower, got dressed, and went to the furniture store, where I spent the rest of the morning doing nothing of particular importance. By the time I got back to the house, Celeste, Clotilde, and my father were seated around the table. I didn't usually eat with my father, because he ate lunch too early, but this time, desperate to know how successful Celeste's visit with the Colonel had been, I sat down at the table with them. However, Celeste, occupied with raising pieces of food to my father's mouth, didn't look at me even once, and it wasn't until my father finished eating and Clotilde took him to lie down, that she could speak to me, and she said I should relax because she'd forced the Colonel to promise he wouldn't report me. I asked her how, and she said that she'd given him a neck massage.

"And that was enough?"

"I promised that I'd give him others."

"Others? How many?"

"I don't know, we didn't set anything up."

She bent down to open the lower cupboard where she kept the dish soap, but I felt like she did this so she wouldn't have to look at me.

"And is he going to pay you for them?" I asked.

"I don't know, Señor Eduardo."

I watched her and I had the impression that their arrangement didn't upset her. I would have never imagined Celeste could have made me jealous. It wasn't exactly my jealousy but my father's, which I shouldered for him since he couldn't feel it for himself because of the condition he was in. At that moment Clotilde came into the kitchen to tell her aunt that she was going home. I left the kitchen and went to my bedroom. My blood was boiling, and I felt like going to the Colonel's house and punching him in the face. But more than anything I was upset with myself, for allowing Celeste to go and visit him. I should have gone, to try to arrive at some agreement and, if we couldn't, to tell him to fuck off and that he could do what he wanted. I wondered how far I'd be willing to go, now that he had the upper hand (the *higher hands*, Father Clark would have said), and how far Celeste would be willing to go to protect me. I hardly knew her at all: The once reserved, passive woman had turned into an effusive and sensual being, who in our visit to the Colonel had taken control of the situation, and she saved me for a second time in the Jiménez brothers' house, reciting from memory the

two Isabel Fraire poems. I saw her again in my father's
bed, embraced by him, but not returning his embrace,
offering her back as if throwing a lifeline to someone
drowning, and that feeling of gratitude and repulsion I'd
found for her returned.

THURSDAY AFTERNOON, just like she told me she'd
do, Celeste went back to the Colonel's house. Clotilde
filled in for her, helped me pot some geraniums and tie
up the bougainvillea guide lines that encircled the porch
columns. I was waiting for Celeste's return and kept
glancing at my watch. At some point I went to her room
to look for the garden trowel, which for some reason we
kept in her closet. Clotilde had left her purse open on
her aunt's bed and I saw that she'd brought her pajamas.
She only brought them when she spent the night at our
house, on those rare occasions Celeste left to visit her
son in the town where he lived. I went back to the yard
and asked her if she was going to spend the night. She
said yes, because Celeste had told her that she probably
wouldn't come back that evening. I almost dropped the
trowel.

"Why didn't she tell me?" I shouted.

Poor Clotilde, who'd never heard me raise my voice,
went pale.

Celeste didn't return until the next day, around
seven in the morning, in fact. I heard her speaking with

her niece in the kitchen, and I was tempted to listen in on the conversation, but I stopped myself. Passing my father's room on my way to the bathroom I saw that he was still asleep, strange for that hour. I imagined that he must have found out from Clotilde that Celeste would be away all night and now he too acted like he was asleep so he wouldn't have to speak with her.

Since I didn't know what to say to Celeste, I decided to have breakfast somewhere else. I didn't go to Sanborns de Piedra, because I'd planned to go there that afternoon, so I decided to go to La Oriental Café, which was on the way to the furniture store, and they made good rolls. I arrived at the furniture store just in time, because there were three customers, two young couples and an elderly gentleman, and Jaime was overwhelmed. I attended to one of the couples—they bought a queen-size bed—and then the elderly man, who flirted with a walnut desk but couldn't bring himself to buy it.

While Jaime attended to the other couple, I dialed Güero's number; he answered immediately. I told him that I wanted to talk to him.

"I can't pay what I owe you yet," he told me.

"That's not why I'm calling. Will five o'clock work, same place as last time?"

He said yes, we hung up, and almost immediately my phone rang again. It was Mario, the Banorte Bank executive whose cubicle was next to Rosario's. He informed me that Regino García, the taxi driver, had just picked up the little bottle of ointment and had left me one hundred pesos. I told him I thought that was strange, because Celeste had made it clear the ointment was a gift.

"Well, the money's here, come by any time."

I told him I'd come by at once, because it was close to where I was going. That wasn't true, but it was an excuse to leave the furniture store and to give Rosario another opportunity to apologize to me.

It took me fifteen minutes to get there, but before I went in to see Mario I looked into Rosario's cubicle. She wasn't there. Mario saw me from his cubicle; he was with a customer and told me that Rosario had gone out and that she'd be back in thirty minutes. He stood up to take his wallet out of his pocket and give me the hundred pesos, but I told him I'd wait until he was free because I wanted to talk to him about my father's mutual fund. That wasn't true; I only wanted to wait around for Rosario to return. Mario sat back down and I took a seat in the adjacent lounge where other customers were awaiting their turn. I grabbed a magazine from the table and a person in front of me exclaimed: "Eduardo Valverde!"

It was Humberto Reséndiz, Amalia's husband. I stood up to shake his hand and he pointed to the chair beside him, wanting me to sit there.

"I'm glad to see you," he told me. "Don't go to the house tomorrow. We called Father Clark yesterday to cancel your reading. He didn't tell you?"

"No. Is your wife ill?"

"Not at all! She's healthier than ever. She finally convinced the owner of El Caracol to host a soiree with music and poetry in honor of Maribel Fraire, and she's running around like a crazy woman getting everything ready."

"Isabel," I corrected.

"What'd you say?" he raised a hand to his ear. Humberto Reséndiz was a little hard of hearing.

"Her name's Isabel, not Maribel."

"Oh, right." He grabbed my arm. "We're counting on you, Eduardo, you won't let us down. We've already talked to Father Clark. There's also going to be music. A mezzo-soprano is going to sing, accompanied by a guitarist. She seems to be a very elegant woman."

"What's her name?"

"Amalia told me, but I forgot."

"It's not Margó Benítez, is it?"

"That one! Do you know her?"

"Yes."

"A very elegant person; Father Clark recommended her."

At that moment a young executive came out of his cubicle and told Humberto Reséndiz that he could come in. Amalia's husband stood up, we hugged, and he told me again that they were counting on me.

I sat back down, picked up the same magazine as before and started to flip through it. I looked at my watch. Rosario hadn't come back and Mario was still with his customer. It seemed absurd to continue waiting for only a hundred pesos. I stood up, put the magazine on the table, and left the bank.

Now, at least, I had something to talk about with Celeste. When I got home, Clotilde had left and Papá was watching a tennis match on TV. Celeste was in the kitchen making lunch, and without any preamble I said, "Mario, the guy from the bank, called me. Remember him?"

"Of course." She stopped chopping the zucchini to listen to me.

"The taxi driver went to pick up the ointment you left for him, and guess what? He left you one hundred pesos."

"But I told him it was free!"

"That's what I told Mario."

She shook her head and went back to what she was doing. I opened the fridge and poured myself a glass of juice. While I was drinking it, she asked me, "Do you want me to go and pick it up?"

"The hundred pesos?"

"Yes, there's no need to bother yourself, Eduardo," she said without looking at me. "I can ask Clotilde to fill in for me some morning."

"All morning to go to the bank and come back? It's only a ten-minute taxi ride."

She blushed and said, "I'd go to the market, too. On Wednesdays there's a street market downtown."

She was lying to me. She wasn't going to any market, especially not one in the center of the city. I wondered if she was falling in love with the Colonel, because I guessed that was why she wanted to go out, to see him, and I imagined her lying next to him, her back to him, held in his arms. I thought my father would have assigned her the three *p*'s: purpose, prowess, and prudence. She'd saved me, no doubt about that, and she continued to save me, because if it wasn't for her, the Colonel would have turned me in, even though he didn't like the police.

"No need to go out for the money, I just went by and picked it up," I told her, and removing my wallet I took out a hundred-peso note, put it on the spice rack, and left the kitchen.

I MADE IT to Sanborns de Piedra by five o'clock sharp. Güero was already there and he'd chosen the same table as the previous time, but he hadn't ordered anything, so I assumed he didn't have a cent on him. When I sat down and he asked about my father, I shook my head and told him that what he was living couldn't be called a life, the pain in his bones was killing him and at times I wanted him to die.

"What about him?" he asked me.

"Him what?"

"Does he want to die?"

"Yes."

"How do you know? Did he tell you?"

"No, but I know."

The waiter approached. He was the same one as the previous time. We ordered a León and an Indio.

"You needed to speak to me?" he asked once the waiter had walked away.

I told him about everything that had happened with Colonel Atarriaga. When I finished, I told him that one of his visits to the pensioner would convince the old goat to abandon his arrogant pretenses with Celeste.

Right then, the waiter brought our beers. Güero poured his own, watching how the foam diminished in volume in his glass.

"I know the Colonel," he told me. "He still has a lot of contacts in the military, and we can't step on that terrain." He pointed at the ceiling, a clear allusion to his superiors.

"No one has to find out," I told him. "You scare the shit out of him and that's all. Celeste would do anything to protect me, and he's taking advantage of that."

"What do you mean?"

"He's making her spend the night with him."

"Is she hot?" he asked.

Güero hadn't met Celeste, because by the time my father got sick, he was no longer welcome in our house.

"No, she's not hot and she's not young, but she gives a really good massage. The old man has become smitten with her."

"They won't let anyone mess with a retired colonel," he said, leaning forward in his chair. "There's a nonaggression pact with them, you know what I mean? Leave it up to that woman. From what you're telling me, she'll know how to handle it."

"And what if she leaves my father for that old dog?" I blurted out.

He glanced around and, lowering his voice, asked me, "Do you want me to kill him? Because I don't see any other way around this business."

The waiter was on the other side of the room, but he was looking at us, to see if he could bring us something else. I took a long swig of beer, almost finishing it. Güero hadn't taken his eyes off mine, waiting for a response, and as I didn't say anything, he took a swig of his beer and then another until he finished his bottle. He stood up and told me he had to go. Then he added, leaning down to me, "If you change your mind, let me know. I'd do it for your father."

"Kill?"

He nodded.

"Even him?" I asked.

"Him who?"

"My father."

He watched me while I took another drink of my beer. He hesitated, then he sat back down.

"Is that what you want?" he asked.

"Don't pay any attention to me, it's just that sometimes I think he'd thank me for it."

"Did he ask you to do it?"

"Of course not. That would be like complaining, and he never complains. Seems like he's lived his life with only one objective: never complain. It's as if that were his mission in life."

"If he hasn't asked you to do it, I can't do anything," he said.

"I know. I just wanted to know."

"Know what?"

"Nothing."

"If you can count on me?"

I lifted the bottle to my mouth and drained it.

"Yes," I replied.

He watched me and I avoided looking at him.

"Leave it up to him," he said as he stood, and he burped.

He seemed confident about what he said, as if my father had already talked to him about the matter. As if everything had already been arranged between them and I didn't have to get involved.

"Leave it up to him." I laughed. "Nothing's up to him these days. Obviously, it's been a long time since you've seen him, Güero."

I had said his name, despite myself. He could interpret that as the slightest gesture of affection, and I tried to erase that impression by taking another swig of my beer, but it was empty, and I thought, I was dealing with Güero after all, my father's first employee, the man who'd helped him get the furniture store on its feet, and I assumed that at some point he'd held me in his arms when I was a child. Then I said, "You were seen with David."

"When?"

"Five or six days ago."

"I haven't seen David for two weeks."

"You were seen with him."

"Where?"

"In El Caracol. You were outside and he was inside."

"What's El Caracol?"

"A used bookstore. It opened a few months ago. It's at the end of Río Mayo."

"I have no idea what you're talking about."

"Seriously?"

"Seriously."

"That means David was with someone else. They described him to me, and I thought it was you."

"And what was David supposed to be doing in a used bookstore? Buying a book? He has a hard enough time reading the order list!"

"The same thing they do to me," I told him.

Güero hesitated for a moment, absorbed my sentence, and sat back down for the second time.

"Are you saying he was making the owner of the bookstore shell out for a payment?"

It was the first time he'd used the words "payment" and "shell out" with me. He was always careful to use euphemisms like "make a contribution," "provide sponsorship," and even "reciprocity."

"Yes, the owner told me; he's a friend," I answered. "He knows I have a furniture store and he called to ask what to do in situations like these. Like I told you, he just opened."

"If what you're saying is true, David's crossed a line."

"What's that supposed to mean?"

"What's it supposed to mean? It means that he's crossed a line, that little fucker. He's done it before and this time they're gonna fuck him up good."

IN A WAY I'd also crossed a line in the house of Margó Benítez, sleeping in her bed and afterward creeping up on Aurelia's naked body in order to make love to her, when I should have left. Even though I didn't do anything reprehensible, I wouldn't have been surprised if Margó never opened the door for me again. I don't know what I'd do if she also dropped out of the home reading program. I still had to complete a quarter of my community service hours and I was running out of listeners. The Jiménez brothers had canceled, the same as Colonel Atarriaga; the Reséndizes had just canceled a reading, and the way things were looking, with Señora Reséndiz launching her career as a patron of the arts, it wasn't at all improbable that they'd follow the example of the others. Regarding the Vigil family, after the rebellion of the non-deaf, of which I was the cause, I wouldn't have been surprised if the priest decided to cut his losses in order to restore the monastic order that reigned in his home before my appearance. I was horrified, imagining the interruption of the home reading program looming over my head, along with my consequent consignment to cleaning the toilets in some government hospital or prison.

When Aurelia opened the door with her customary smile, there was not the slightest hint of malice in her eyes, as if nothing had happened between us during my previous visit. At the far end of the living room, in her wheelchair, Margó was speaking with Rómulo Esparza, her voice coach. Her hair was loose and she looked gorgeous. Rómulo Esparza and I shook hands, coldly, which didn't go unnoticed by Margó. With her hair down like that she reminded me of the photograph on her bedside table, and I wondered if she'd untied it on purpose, as a way to tell me that she knew that I'd slept in her bedroom. Maybe it was true that she'd concocted everything so I'd see her photograph when I woke in her bed and that I'd know the magnitude of the beauty she was capable of. I looked at Rómulo Esparza, whose obsequious, almost pretentious mannerisms appeared to be proof of his passion for the owner of the house. I was so stunned by Margó's change in appearance that I forgot to shake her hand.

"Please be seated, Eduardo," she told me, addressing me formally once again in front of her voice coach, and that hint of collusion with me produced an inner meltdown. "Did someone cut out your tongue? Why aren't you saying anything?"

At that point, Aurelia brought a cup of coffee for me from the kitchen. Margo's cup and that of the voice coach were empty on the center table where there was also a plate of cookies.

"Help yourself to a cookie," Margó said. "Maestro Esparza brought them and they're delicious. Did you know that I've been asked to sing at the event in honor of Isabel Fraire?"

"Yes, Humberto Reséndiz told me. Congratulations."

"You should congratulate Maestro Esparza as well. Without him, I'd never dare to do such a thing."

I congratulated Rómulo Esparza, who thanked me by nodding his head.

Margó asked if I could help them adapt some lines by Isabel Fraire to a melody Maestro Esparza had composed. She'd thought of the poem about skin I'd read to her.

Here we go again with the skin poem! It seemed as if it were the only poem Isabel Fraire had written.

"Tatis Reséndiz is going to recite that poem," I told them.

"That's not a problem at all, quite the opposite," Rómulo Esparza said. "The audience will enjoy a double performance of the same poem. Do you have it with you?"

I didn't have the book, but I did have the page where I'd copied it out by hand so I could read it to Margó. I opened my briefcase and gave the sheet of paper to the maestro.

The truth was that I didn't give a damn about any of this. I and no one else was responsible for the turn things had taken, when I fell into the declamatory webs Amalia Reséndiz wove. I should have refused when the couple asked my permission to invite their friends to my readings. From that moment on everything had become overblown and vulgar. I remembered my father stammering when he read Isabel Fraire's lines and I felt like a fraud twice over. Poor Isabel Fraire, hardly read when she was alive and abused in death.

Rómulo Esparza, finishing reading over the skin poem, moved his head to indicate that he was profoundly affected.

"Sublime!" he uttered with a sigh. "I'm going to copy it down right now," and he took out a fountain pen and started to copy it on the back of a piece of sheet music.

"I really don't think it's such a good idea to sing Isabel Fraire's poems," I said, unable to contain myself.

"Why not?" Margó asked.

"Her lines should be whispered," I said, "almost mumbled, not sung."

"You didn't mumble at all when you read them to me the first time, Eduardo; you even made me cry."

I didn't know how to respond, and fortunately Aurelia came in again to remove the empty cups her employer and Rómulo Esparza had left on the table. I looked at her eyes for a sign of our shared afternoon, but her smile was as pristine as the porcelain coffee service, identical to the smiles she always bestowed upon me. She went back to the kitchen and Rómulo Esparza asked for permission to use the bathroom, thereby leaving Margó and me alone.

"Drink your coffee, it's getting cold," she said, lowering her voice and once again addressing me informally.

"You look beautiful with your hair down," I told her, and I took a sip of my coffee.

"Thank you." She smiled.

"Thank you for the coffee the other day, when you weren't at home."

"I didn't have a chance to tell you beforehand. Forgive me if I made you come in vain."

"I didn't come in vain," I told her, and I hesitated, doubting whether to tell her I'd slept in her bedroom and contemplated the photograph of her in the bathing suit, but the risk of somehow compromising Aurelia made me restrain myself.

"Is something wrong?" I asked, because she seemed pensive.

"No."

Her dry reply made me insist: "What's going on?"

"Nothing."

She looked down, focused on the rug. The coffee table stood between us and I got to my feet, thinking I would sidestep that obstacle and embrace her and kiss her, but at that moment the bathroom door opened and Rómulo Esparza returned to the living room, rubbing his hands.

"Have you convinced our friend Eduardo that we can indeed sing Isolda Fraire's poems?" he asked the owner of the house.

"Isabel," I corrected.

"We were talking about something else," Margó said.

Rómulo Esparza removed his guitar from its case, tuned it, and hummed a melody, then he looked at the poem he'd just copied, and he started to set the lines to the melody, looking at Margó, who looked back at him. They understood each other perfectly and I felt jealous of the voice coach, who clearly had an influence on the owner of the house. Margó didn't sing a single note; instead she merely hummed the lines Rómulo Esparza indicated to her, softly. I had the feeling that my presence was making her self-conscious, that's why I stood up and went to the kitchen for a glass of water. When she saw me enter, Aurelia's daughter ran to a corner to hide, I suppose because she wasn't used to seeing me there, and Aurelia, typical of her, smiled at me excessively. I asked her for a glass of water. The girl watched me, intrigued, from her corner, while her mother gave me a glass of water on a little plate, and I asked her under my breath if she'd put something in my tequila, more than anything to remind her of our encounter a few days before and to assure myself that she hadn't forgotten about it, but I was struck again by her unbridled smile, which made me wonder again if she wasn't a little crazy. The girl ran to hide under the table and from there she watched me, a picaresque smile on her face, which was a carbon copy of her mother's. In the living room Rómulo Esparza was marking a beat and we heard a guitar chord.

"No, that's too high, go down an octave," Margó told him, and insisted, "down, down."

Fed up with Aurelia's smiling face, I obeyed Margo's instructions and I went down, that is I got under the table, beside the girl, who covered her mouth to stifle her giggles. Aurelia bent down and shook her daughter, which frightened her and made her cry out, and then she straightened up again and left us alone in that imaginary cave. I watched Aurelia's legs as she moved around the kitchen and I regretted not making love to her in her room the week before. That was what she wanted, otherwise she wouldn't have taken off her clothes. My member came alive remembering her prominent ass, with just that right amount of cellulite that I like so much and that makes an ass appear to have been touched by many hands. The girl suddenly became serious, as if she wondered what we were doing there, which was the same thing I was asking myself. The only one who seemed to think it was normal was Aurelia, who began to hum while she bustled about the kitchen. I supposed that she was happy because the friend of her employer, the distinguished young man who came to the house to read books, was under the table playing with her daughter. It suddenly occurred to me that children that age are meant to be kissed, so I reached for the girl's face and kissed her on the cheek, but my member was still hard and, embarrassed, I looked away from her, focusing on a vague point until my erection subsided. Then I kissed her again, thinking it had been ages since I'd kissed a child. After Mamá's death I'd lived among wrinkles and decline, and once I'd started reading for people in their homes that landscape of flabby skin had expanded and become more pronounced. Even Gladis, who'd always been pure oxygen for me, was growing older before my eyes. Were there home readers for children, like there were for the retired and infirm? A job like that would best be done under tables. I kissed Aurelia's daughter again and asked her if she enjoyed her visit to Valle de Bravo. Her mother, hearing my question, bent down and told her, "Tell him yes, that you liked it a lot."

The girl looked like she didn't understand, and Aurelia became enraged. "Come on, you stupid girl, tell him you liked it!"

She was frightened, started to cry, and I defended her.

"Don't yell at her," I told Aurelia, and held the child in my arms, but she broke loose, as frightened of my arms as she was of her mother's behavior.

"Why is Griselda crying?" Margó shouted from the living room.

Aurelia grabbed her daughter roughly by the hand.

"It's nothing, señora," she said, and she left the kitchen with the girl, taking her to her room. Rómulo Esparza and Margó said something I didn't hear, and I assumed they were talking about me. I thought she would call for me, but she didn't, and I waited for her to enter the kitchen in her wheelchair and see me there, under the table. I'd tell her that I wanted to hear her sing and that I'd come to the kitchen because I thought that she felt self-conscious in front of me in the living room. Under the table? she'd ask me, and I was overwhelmed by the feeling of how ridiculous my situation was. I imagined Father Clark coming into the kitchen suddenly and saying, "I'm glad to see you, Eduardo," and sitting next to me, under the table, to tell me something of great importance. Leaving there he'd slam the table into the wall, inciting Margó's rage. I started to laugh. I didn't feel like moving, as if I'd found my true place in the world, and that made me laugh even harder. I expected nothing, absolutely nothing, and that was a revelation, in its own way. I heard another guitar chord emanating from the living room. All of a sudden everything annoyed me. Rómulo Esparza's simple presence with his toilet etiquette made me sick. I was expected to complete one hour of home reading, but I was not obliged to listen to their rehearsal. Then the girl reappeared, looked at me, laughed, and left again. Reluctantly, I got up and went back to the living room, where Rómulo Esparza was putting his guitar back in its case. The rehearsal had come to an end and both of them avoided looking at me. Margó was visibly furious with me and I prudently decided not to have her sign my visitation form. She and Rómulo Esparza said goodbye with a kiss on the cheek, then she turned her wheelchair and rolled down the hall without saying goodbye to me. I picked up my briefcase and followed Rómulo Esparza to the door. He opened it and we left together. Once we were on the street he asked where I'd parked my car and I told him I'd come on foot.

"Me too," he said.

We were heading in opposite directions, but I decided to walk to the corner with him because I needed human companionship and, while we walked, I noticed that his stuffy-looking mannerisms had disappeared. We moved forward shoulder to shoulder due to the narrow sidewalk, rubbing into each other with each step and at no time did he attempt to move away from me. I felt revived by this unexpected physical contact. I'd misjudged him, I thought. He earned his living giving private lessons and perhaps his calculated mannerisms were a tool of his trade. I wanted to initiate a friendly conversation to show him there were no hard feelings and that he could trust me, but the noise from the traffic was unbearable. We walked as if we were fleeing a conflagration. I wished he would have stopped suddenly and asked me, "What's wrong with you, Eduardo? Why'd you go to the kitchen and hide under the table? Didn't you see how your actions affected our dear Margó, who loves you so much?" I was prepared to receive his heartfelt complaints, as long as they were made in the spirit of friendship. I would have loved for him to tell me, "Go back to Margó's house right now and ask her to forgive you, get down on your knees if you have to and kiss her hands. She adores you, Eduardo, she's told me as much. She didn't get one note right because of how distraught she was, didn't you notice? That's why we ended our rehearsal so early." I'd hug him, thank him for his advice, ask him to forgive my arrogance, and afterward I'd run back to Margó's house and do exactly what that good man had asked me to do. I saw myself weeping on my knees while I kissed her hands, praising her kindness and her skin as if they were one and the same thing. *Your skin, your skin, Margó, does anything else matter?* I'd tell her. But we'd already reached the corner, where our paths diverged, without speaking a single word to each other. Rómulo Esparza extended his hand and he didn't even thank me for walking with him. We shook hands coldly and I watched him cross the street, moving away through the crowd and the roaring traffic. That was our City of Eternal Spring!

THAT NIGHT I looked for all the Isabel Fraire books Papá owned. There were three and only one of them was of her own poetry, the same one I'd bought from Abigael Martínez. There was a small volume of her translations of English-speaking poets and a book of essays titled *North American Thinkers of the XX Century*. On the back cover of this last one there was an author photo. You could see a woman with a wide face, long black hair hanging down and hiding part of it, her features vaguely reminding me of a Sioux Indian, and she had a thick, sensual mouth that contrasted with the serenity of her gaze. It wasn't a face one would easily forget, even if you couldn't say she was beautiful. The picture had been taken nine years before. None of these books had an inscription. I opened them, searching among the pages for some indication of the friendship between her and my father, like a postcard, or some scrap of paper with writing on it, but I didn't find anything. I thought that, had they been lovers, she would have left the smallest written clue in one of these books, even if it had been an unoriginal inscription, devised so it wouldn't raise any suspicions in my mother. I looked at the picture again, trying to imagine how those inquisitive-looking eyes would settle on my father's, and I thought it was idiotic to presume there'd been something between the two of them. What would he, an unassuming furniture-store owner who liked poetry, have talked about with one of the most talented poets in the country, whose lines, more whimsical than obedient to any kind of linear order, seemed to boil over the page? She tended to fall off ladders, Abigael had told me over breakfast at Sanborns, and I suspected, by how he said it, that he was in love with her himself, though she didn't love him in return. He also told me that his wife wrote poems and from time to time, at Isabel's insistence, she showed them to her, and though Isabel liked them, his wife never had the nerve to publish anything during her lifetime.

The telephone rang. It was Margó. As soon as I heard her voice I knew she was still upset with me. She reproached me for how rudely I'd behaved with her and Rómulo Esparza, leaving them alone in the living room to go to the kitchen with Aurelia. But what hurt her the most, she added, was that I would have doubted her ability to sing Isabel Fraire's poetry. I told her that I hadn't said that, but that her poetry in particular, in my opinion, was not the most suitable to be sung, and I added: "I went to the kitchen because I felt like my presence made you feel self-conscious about singing and I was dying to listen to you."

My words hit their mark, because she was quiet, although she recovered immediately. "Why do you always run away?"

"I didn't run away," I told her, "I went for a glass of water and I ended up playing with Aurelia's daughter. It's been years since I've played with a child."

"Aurelia told me she was crying because you kissed her."

"That's not true, she was crying because her mother shouted at her."

"You kissed her?" she asked.

"Yes, we were under the table and I kissed her."

"Her mother didn't like that."

"Why?"

"She didn't like it; both of you were under the table and she couldn't see you."

I could feel the blood in my arms starting to heat up, and I remembered that Aurelia had hummed cheerfully while Griselda and I were under the table.

"Of course she could, all she had to do was bend over to see us!" I shouted. "What's she insinuating?"

Celeste, who'd been in the kitchen, looked into the living room when she heard me shout.

"Why aren't you saying anything?" I asked Margó, lowering my voice.

"I've never heard you shout," she said, as if my shouting had revealed God knows what kind of dark twists and turns in my personality to her. I suspected that she was thinking about my accident, or the misfortune, as Celeste called it, asking herself if things had occurred the way I'd told her, and I regretted opening up to her like that.

"What are you thinking about?" I asked, but she'd already hung up.

FATHER CLARK called me in the morning. I imagined him rocking back in his chair, from which he would stand at some point with an abrupt push that would add a new dent to his office wall. I'm glad I caught you, he told me, and he explained that his organization was going to finance a large part of the expenses for the Isabel Fraire tribute. Part of those expenses included wages for an assistant who would help out with a little bit of everything, such as keeping an eye on the sound system so it worked properly and even making sure no one stole books from the shelves, taking advantage of the general bustle in the bookstore during the event, and he told me that I would be this assistant.

"Me? What do I have to do with any of this?" I snapped.

He told me they'd count it as part of my community service, and considering the numerous desertions from my reading program, I should be grateful.

"Numerous? I only know about two, the Jiménez brothers and Colonel Atarriaga."

"Now there are three. Margó Benítez called me last night to tell me she's canceling, too."

I felt like I was going to faint.

"Margó? How come?" I asked.

"She says you don't pay attention to what you're reading. The same thing Carlos Jiménez told me, by the way."

I looked at the wall, the infinite living-room wall, and everything Father Clark said after that sounded like a distant buzz. I heard a sharp noise and I knew he'd stood up from his swivel chair. Shortly after that we hung up. I hadn't followed one word he'd said. I looked at the wall again. Right then, the phone rang. It was my sister. She called to chew me out for my negligent behavior. Her Bible circle friend, tired of waiting in vain for me to call her back, had bought her futon from another furniture store. I chewed her out for not warning me I'd be Abigael Martínez's assistant during the poetry soiree in El Caracol.

"I thought you were okay with that," she said.

"Father Clark just called to tell me, and he didn't ask if I was okay with it."

"It's my understanding that it counts as part of your community service."

"My community service is reading in people's homes, not serving as some lackey for cultural soirees."

"You're not going to be anyone's lackey, Edu. Father Clark even thought you might say a few words about Isabel Fraire."

I'm sure that was what the priest had told me while I was watching the wall.

"I have nothing to say about Isabel Fraire," I told her, "and don't call me Edu."

I hated it when she called me Edu. She had a boyfriend named Eduardo like me, and she called him Edu, I think so she could differentiate the two of us, but from time to time she'd use the same moniker with me.

"You could at least say that she was my papi's favorite poet. He'd like that."

"Who would?"

"My papi would."

It annoyed me that she called him "papi," and especially that she said "my papi" when she was talking to me, her brother, as if we had two different papis.

"So, you're thinking of taking Papá to the soiree?" I asked her.

"Of course. It's going to make him really happy. He always said that Isabel Fraire deserved greater recognition than she received during her lifetime, and we're giving it to her."

We're giving it to her. She talked as if she were on the organizing committee.

"The soiree's going to be an embarrassment," I said. "You didn't stick around to listen to the people who read in the Reséndizes' house, but I did."

"Amalia Reséndiz told me that the readings were stunning...just that...you were the only one who was a little sloppy."

"She told you that? That my reading was sloppy?"

"A little."

"Of course I was sloppy," I exclaimed. "That idiot Tatis took my book and I had to improvise."

"Who's Tatis?"

"Amalia Reséndiz's niece, the gangster's girlfriend."

"What gangster?"

"The idiot's, I meant to say."

"You're pretty upset," she said, and I admitted that I was. She asked me why and I told her that Margó Benítez had just dropped out of the home reading program.

"Who's she?"

"My best listener," I told her.

"Why'd she drop out?"

"Because she doesn't like how I read. That's what she told Father Clark, but that's not the real reason."

"So what is?"

"I did something stupid."

"What'd you do?"

I looked at the wall again. Where to start? I told her bluntly, "I played hide-and-seek with the maid's daughter."

There was a brief silence and then Ofelia exclaimed, "You played hide-and-seek with the maid's daughter, instead of reading?"

"No, I went to the kitchen for a glass of water and I hid under the table with the girl."

"Why?"

"Because I felt like it."

"For how long?"

"A few minutes. Margó was in the living room rehearsing an aria from an opera. She's the mezzo-soprano who's going to sing at the poetry soiree honoring Isabel Fraire. I kissed the girl and her mother got upset."

"How did you kiss her?"

"How do you think I kissed a five-year-old girl? On the cheek."

"I don't understand any of this," Ofelia acquiesced.

"Forget about it," I told her.

"Father Clark told me that someone else from your group canceled."

"Colonel Atarriaga. A nefarious guy, worse than the Jiménez brothers."

"Why are all of them canceling your readings?"

"Now all I need for you to do is psychoanalyze me."

"I don't understand why you hid under a table with a little girl."

"Because we were playing, something you don't do anymore."

"You're going to start attacking me now?"

"I'm upset. The thing with Margó messed me up."

"What do you mean? Why'd it mess you up?"

"Because I didn't deserve it!"

"It's okay, you have to calm down."

"I know."

"Do you want me to come over?"

"No, I'm fine."

"I can be there in fifteen minutes, I just need to get dressed."

"No, really Ofelia, I'm fine. It took me by surprise, but I'm fine."

There was silence.

"Did you fall in love with that woman, Edu?" she asked.

"Don't call me Edu," I told her.

She was quiet and I looked at the wall again. Celeste came into the living room to get something from the table and I was struck by the way she moved. Something about her flowed with unprecedented assurance, as if she'd come to terms with that body she'd always kept muted, and I was certain that she'd slept with Colonel Atarriaga.

I WAS IN SANBORNS DE PIEDRA having some rolls for breakfast a little after eleven when Jaime called my cell phone to tell me he'd just been robbed.

"It was the tall guy who always waits outside when Güero comes by to pick up the money," he said.

"David?"

"I don't know his name. He took fourteen thousand pesos from the cash register. He had a gun."

I asked him if he was okay and he said yes. The guy hadn't touched him. I left a two-hundred-peso note on the table, enough for three orders of rolls, and I told Gladis that she could give me my change later. Outside I stopped the first taxi I saw. On the way to the furniture store I thought I should have seen this coming. If they were going to cut this guy's throat, as Güero had warned me, it was really only natural that he'd rob us, because he was going to need money to escape and get as far away as possible.

It took me ten minutes to get to the furniture store and Jaime was at the door waiting for me. He looked really calm.

"Are you okay?" I asked, and he said that he was. I went directly to the cash register, opened it and saw that there was only one twenty-peso note and a few coins. I asked if the guy had been alone.

"No, he was with some other guy I've never seen before who kept watch at the door." He explained that an hour earlier he'd sold the Olympia desk made out of walnut for twelve thousand five hundred pesos, and the customer had paid in cash. That's why there was so much money in the register.

"If he'd come an hour earlier, he'd only have taken a thousand pesos," he said.

He told me how it all happened, though there wasn't much to tell. David didn't even have to pull out his pistol; he only had to show it to Jaime, then order him to open the cash register. Since they were the only ones in the store, everything had happened really fast and without any violence.

Jaime sat down on one of the tartan sofas. The fact that he sat on an item we wanted to sell showed me how nervous and exhausted he was, and I was afraid his next words would be that he was quitting.

"Take the rest of the day off," I told him.

"What for?"

"You've had a rough morning, go to the movies with your wife."

"With my wife? I'm better off here."

I sat in front of him on one of the Inoka chairs. For the first time in my life I felt like I was the owner of the furniture store, that I was the boss and Jaime was my employee. Güero was right. Guys like David were capable of anything. We'd been lucky we'd sold the walnut desk an hour before. Maybe those fourteen thousand pesos had saved Jaime's life or kept them from setting the furniture store on fire. But I didn't tell Jaime that. I only told him that this guy, David, had crossed a line. He asked me what that meant and I told him that he was shaking people down on the side without giving a cut to his bosses; they'd found out about it and he'd fled with his crony, but not before "reviewing" the businesses under his protection one more time to get as much money as he could.

"He burned his bridges, you understand? We won't see his face again, you can be sure of that," and I added, repeating Güero's phrase: "They're gonna fuck him up good."

I don't know if he heard me. He looked into the distance and I imagined that he was thinking about how miserable his life as our employee had been, his job future uncertain, and how he had to put up with criminals. I knew he didn't have any friends. I could see that from the few conversations we had from time to time, and there was something in his face that rejected friendship, a kind of greedy sneer affixed there resulting from his disregard for anything he found inconvenient. He was a violent pushover, in a manner of speaking, even capable of some act of courage as long as it didn't interfere with his privacy.

I remembered that I'd brought Isabel Fraire's book about twentieth-century North American thinkers with me, the one with her photograph, and I went to pull it out of my briefcase to show her picture to Jaime. I asked him if he'd ever seen that woman in the furniture store; he looked at the picture and asked me who she was.

"A friend of my father's."

"Does she have something to do with the robbery?" he asked.

"Of course not. She's a poet. You don't remember ever seeing her here?"

He looked at the picture again and said no. I put the book back in my briefcase, and I thought I should ask Güero about it. Isabel had fallen off the ladder six or seven years ago, during the time Güero worked with my father. If she'd come to the furniture store, he'd have to remember her, because the book photo was from around that time and Isabel's face wasn't easy to forget.

I told Jaime that we weren't going to report anything to the police, because then it would come out that David had been blackmailing us for more than a year and it was absolutely necessary that my sister not find out about any of this.

"You should have never made that deal," he said.

"Who said I made any deal?" I asked him, wanting to kick his ass.

OFELIA WENT TO THE HOUSE to go over some bills with Celeste and have Papá try on the pants and jacket she wanted him to wear that Friday night to El Caracol. It seemed like an excessively formal outfit for a poetry recital, but I didn't say anything. Between the two of them, they dressed and undressed him several times; because my father had lost so much weight during the previous year he didn't have one suit that fit him well, all of them were baggy and made him look like a scarecrow. First, he tried on a light gray combination, then a darker gray one, and, finally, a suit that was almost black. I wondered if that trajectory from light to dark didn't somehow reflect my sister's unconscious desire to see him dead.

I spent the first part of Friday morning in the bookstore, working with Abigael to move stacks of books against the walls in order to clear an area where we could set up the chairs and a podium. I remembered two decent-sized pine bookcases I'd had in storage in the furniture store warehouse for quite a while, because they'd turned out to be defective, and I asked him if he wanted them. He said he did, and when I offered to bring them over so the bookstore would look a little more pleasant for the recital, without those stacks of books piled against the walls that gave the place an unkempt appearance, he accepted enthusiastically and asked how we'd get them to the store.

"With the delivery truck we have at the furniture store," I answered, "but you'll have to drive because my license was taken away."

"I don't know how to drive," he said, and he wanted to know why it had been taken away.

"It's a long story."

I called Father Clark and explained that we needed a driver who could help us load a few bookcases I was keeping in the furniture store warehouse and transport them in my truck so the bookstore would look a little more inviting for the evening's event. He asked me if it wasn't a little late to be doing all that work, and I replied that there were so many books stacked against the walls that it made the place look sloppy.

"That seems reasonable to me," he said. "Let me see if I can enlist Efrén, our driver."

Ten minutes later Efrén called me. I arranged to
meet him at the furniture store, and I took a taxi to save
time. He arrived almost immediately after I did. He
was a young and portly man; we went to the warehouse,
which is in the basement of the store, and between us
we carried the two pine bookcases up the stairs, loaded
them into the truck, and tied them down.

The whole day was like that: go up, get down,
load, and move. I discovered how much I missed being
engrossed in a purely physical task. When we arrived
at the bookstore Abigael was moving the piles of books
away from the wall, where we'd placed them an hour
earlier. Efrén and I helped him, and the walls were
finally empty enough to hold the bookcases. They
fascinated Abigael and he asked me what was wrong
with them. We looked them over, we didn't find any
abnormalities, and I wondered if I'd brought the wrong
ones. Efrén and I understood each other immediately.
He grasped the urgency of the situation and offered
to help us with whatever we needed. I asked him if he
knew how to drill holes and sink wall anchors so we
could attach the bookcases to the walls, and he said yes.
While he got to work, Abigael and I tested the sound
system Father Clark had provided: two microphones and
a speaker. The truth is that I was the one who tested it,
because Abigael had to attend to a couple of customers.
The delivery truck with the rented chairs arrived at

midday and I told the guys to stack them in a corner. By that time it was clear that I was the one coordinating operations, because Abigael had to deal with the occasional customer who came into the store and Efrén was grappling with the drill, his use of which, incidentally, appeared to be less than competent. I almost called Filiberto, the carpenter I always use, so he could attach the bookcases to the walls, but we were running short on time so I let Efrén manage as best he could. Because there was a faulty connection in the microphones, I went to a lamp store two blocks away to see if someone could help me out. I knew the owner, he was a friend of Papá's, and he promised to send his assistant when he returned from a delivery. I went back to the bookstore and Abigael told me that Father Clark had just called and he wanted to speak with me. I called him back. He only wanted to know how everything was going and I listed all the tasks that still remained to be done. He asked if I thought we'd finish in time and I said, "I think so, but with so many things left to do, I'd rather not read tonight."

"Do not worry, Amalia Reséndiz gave me the list of those who are going to read and you are not on it."

Far from feeling relieved, I loathed her. She'd taken me off the list of readers after my sloppy performance at her house and I could almost swear she'd suggested that Father Clark use me as the stagehand for the event even though I was the driving force behind those poetic soirees. I deserved it.

"Ofelia told me that you'd like me to say a few words about Isabel Fraire," I told the priest, remembering what my sister had said.

"Yes, but I consulted Amalia Reséndiz and she thinks it is not appropriate."

"Fine," I snapped.

We hung up. The soiree was in honor of a poet no one knew anything about and, nevertheless, saying a few words about her seemed to be inappropriate. I should have said to hell with everything, but I couldn't be rebellious with three people already having dropped out of the home reading program. The possibility of cleaning toilets in the public hospital terrified me.

Efrén finally got one of the bookcases attached to the wall. I started to fill it with books, but I had to stop halfway through, because it was getting late, I was sweaty, and I needed to go home and take a shower and change my clothes. When I told Abigael, he motioned me over to the cash register. He opened the top drawer of the small dresser beneath it and told me to take a look. It was a black pistol with a mother-of-pearl handle.

"I just bought it, it's a Beretta, an automatic," he said lowering his voice.

"What do you need that for?"

"One never knows."

"Is it legal?"

"More legal than your birth certificate."

He raised his finger to his lips as if it were our little secret and closed the drawer.

"Do you know how to use it?" I asked him.

"I'm taking lessons at a shooting range, not far from here. We should go together sometime. It would be a good idea for you to have one around, too."

I nodded, because maybe he was right. I told him we'd see each other later, left the store, and went home.

Ofelia had taken my father and Celeste to her house to eat, planning to leave for the bookstore from there, which meant there was no one in the house, something completely unusual, and I couldn't help thinking that it would be like this when Papá died and I let Celeste go. I couldn't imagine living alone inside those walls where I'd spent my whole life. Would I continue to go to Sanborns de Piedra, living a life of seclusion, or, the other extreme, would I host parties and soirees like the Reséndiz couple did?

After I showered, I changed shirts, but I put on the same jeans I'd been wearing to avoid being called to the stage by Amalia Reséndiz or Father Clark to replace some reader at the last minute. I went to the kitchen to make myself a sandwich and a cup of coffee. While the coffeepot was heating on the stove I went into Celeste's room and opened a drawer in her nightstand and went through her chest of drawers and closet, looking for a letter, a picture, some object related to Colonel Atarriaga, something to indicate the level of intimacy between them. But I didn't find anything. I went back to the kitchen, ate my sandwich, drank my coffee, left the house, and hailed a taxi.

When I got to the bookstore there were already a lot of people and I was afraid there wouldn't be enough chairs. We'd done everything humanly possible to give the place an agreeable appearance: the bookcases lined with books looked imposing, and thanks to them the bookstore seemed more elegant, even classy. However, Efrén hadn't shelved the books correctly; they were sticking out too far, on the edge of each shelf, and I pointed this out to Abigael.

"They're like that because we had to make two rows," he told me. "They wouldn't fit in a single row."

I had a bad feeling about that and I went for a closer look to make sure. The excessive weight of the extra books, combined with Efrén's shoddy work with the drill, had caused the lag screws that attached the bookcases to the wall to emerge from the wall anchors a few millimeters, therefore jeopardizing the overall stability of the bookcases. In fact, one of them had already started to draw away from the wall a little at the top. I asked Abigael where Efrén was and he told me he'd gone to pick up a group of elderly people from Father Clark's Christian organization.

"The bookcases aren't fastened to the wall very well and they could fall over; we should take down the second row of books to lighten up the shelves," I told him.

"I can't, I'm busy at the cash register, you do it," he told me.

"I just took a shower," I objected.

"So once Efrén comes back, we'll tell him to do it."

A young man approached to ask about a book and Abigael led him to the back of the bookstore, down the long corridor that now, thanks to my bookcases, seemed spacious. Maybe because of that I remembered these two lines: "There are avenues so wide, / that crossing them becomes another avenue," and when Abigael returned to where I was standing, I recited them and asked if he was familiar with them. I saw him turn pale; he looked at me as if I were joking and asked how I knew those lines. I told him I wasn't sure, but I'd probably heard them from my father.

"That's one of my wife's poems," he said lowering his voice and staring at me. A silent telegram crossed between us. He seemed to be waiting for me to explain. I didn't say anything, but I felt a profound disappointment when I realized that Isabel Fraire and my father hadn't known each other and that he'd become fond of Isabel's poetry thanks to Abigael Martínez's wife, and it was because of her that my father's phrase, the one about our city not having a soul, only swimming pools, had come to Isabel Fraire's ears.

"My wife's name was Ivonne," Abigael told me, studying my reaction to that name, a name I'd never once heard cross my father's lips. Was he hoping that Papá would discuss his love affairs with his family?

"I've never heard him say that name before," I told him.

"Tell me the truth," he insisted, coming so close his face was almost touching mine. He had bad breath. He was pleading with me, in spite of his gruffness, and I saw a man tormented by jealousy, even after the death of his wife, whom I imagined had been taller than him, with black hair and a sensuous mouth, a mix of Margó Benítez and Isabel Fraire.

"I swear," I told him, holding my breath so I wouldn't have to smell his.

He moved his hand to his pocket and took out his wallet. I assumed he wanted to show me a photo of his wife, but he changed his mind, put his wallet back, and moved away, calming himself down. I could have left then, but I lacked the courage to walk out on everything a little less than half an hour before the soiree began. Anyway, my father was going to arrive in a few minutes and I was tormented by the thought of Abigael's Beretta in the drawer beneath the cash register. I didn't know what the man was capable of. At that moment a customer approached to ask him for a book, he said to follow him, and I took that opportunity to sneak way to the other side of the bookstore. I took out my cell phone and called Ofelia, who told me she was on her way with

Celeste and my father. I told her it wasn't such a good idea to bring Papá.

"Here we go again! I think we've already talked about that."

"Yes, but I've just discovered something."

"What? Speak louder."

"I can't shout," I told her.

"I can't hear you."

The call dropped and I had to hang up. I looked around for Abigael, who was at the cash register, where a modest line had formed, something never before seen in that bookstore. Other people wandered around the shop looking at books and thumbing through their pages. I went back to the bookcases, where a few customers were browsing the shelves, and I leaned against the most dangerous one to secure it against the wall.

People continued to arrive and Abigael couldn't keep up with the sales. Father Clark came in and, when he saw me, came straight over. I noticed his shoes had recently been shined.

"I am glad to see you, Eduardo," he said, turning to look around the whole bookstore. "I am going to be the master of ceremonies. Amalia Reséndiz asked me to. The readers will come in when everything is ready. I want to tell you something," and he took me by the arm to steer me to the corner, but I didn't let him move me, so I wouldn't be separated from the bookcases. He was surprised by my resistance and I told him the truth:

"This could fall over at any minute, and I'd rather stand here so I can hold it up."

I don't think he understood me, but he said, "That seems reasonable to me," and then went on to tell me about David, Tatis Reséndiz's boyfriend, who'd disappeared the previous afternoon. Tatis had received a message from him that morning telling her not to look for him and that she should be careful.

"Careful of what?" I asked.

"We do not know. The poor woman will not stop crying."

I thought he was going to ask me to read in her place and I got out in front of that: "Look how I'm dressed, Father, and I haven't prepared anything. I didn't even bring my Isabel Fraire book. Beyond that, I'm worried about this bookcase. Someone has to stay here and keep an eye on it."

"No one is asking you to read, Edu."

"Please, don't call me Edu."

"Your sister calls you Edu."

"I know, I've asked her not to a thousand times and she still calls me Edu."

"Understood. I am not going to ask you to read in her place, Eduardo, Tatis is a professional and she will do it, no matter what happens," he said.

A professional screamer, I thought to myself.

He leaned against the bookcases I was holding up with my body, and I was afraid one of his sudden movements would pop it out of the wall. He specialized in damaging walls.

"Don't lean on the bookcase, Father," I told him. He didn't understand and I had to tell him again.

He stepped away from it and, in a hushed voice, said, "I have been told something I do not like, Edu...excuse me, Eduardo," and he informed me that this David character, apparently, had been meddling in some dirty business.

"What you mean to say is that he's a criminal?"

"Something like that, and they are looking for him."

"The police?"

"No, the chiffchaff like him."

"Riffraff," I corrected.

"Do not tell Tatis about this."

At that moment, someone called to him from the door and he told me, "I will be right back and I will tell you more."

But we didn't have an opportunity to keep talking because a small blur of elderly people, led by Efrén, entered, some in wheelchairs, others with walkers, and Father Clark had to coordinate how to accommodate them in the available space. The walker users were seated in the last row of chairs and those who were in the wheelchairs were put in front of the stage, which provoked the discontent of the first ones, who protested what they considered an unjust act. Seeing that the elderly contingent had already been seated, the people

who'd been roaming around looking at books decided
to take their seats as well and the room filled to near
capacity in less than a minute. I tried to get Efrén's
attention to ask him to help me remove the second row of
books from the shelves, but I saw that the disgruntlement
rippling through the elderly in the last row occupied him
completely, and between him and Father Clark they were
unable to make any progress calming the complainers
down. Right then, another elderly man in a wheelchair
entered. It was my father, pushed by Celeste. They passed
in front of Abigael, who didn't see them because he was
at the register ringing up a customer. I raised my hand
to catch Celeste's attention and pointed to a place at the
end of the row formed by the wheelchair gang; it would
be more difficult for Abigael to see Papá there. Celeste
wheeled him over and stood beside him. I motioned for
her to come to where I was.

"And Ofelia?" I whispered in her ear.

"She's parking the car."

"Is my father wearing a diaper?"

"Of course."

I looked at Papá, who looked back at me without
recognizing me. Everything must have seemed so strange
to him in that space crowded with people. At least a
year had passed since he'd left the house and worn
ordinary clothes. He was looking for Celeste, who was
beside me, and he had that drowning-man expression
I'd seen in his eyes when he'd tried to recite Isabel

Fraire's poem from memory. His eyes lingered on her, but Celeste, mesmerized by the excitement that prevailed in the bookstore, wasn't paying attention to him. She was wearing the same Indian shawl as the last time we went out, and it occurred to me that this garment somehow changed her inwardly, transformed her into someone else.

"Go back to him, he's looking for you," I told her, and in the self-sacrificing way she approached my father I saw that her days in our house were numbered, and I hoped once again that Papá would die sooner rather than later.

Then another wheelchair appeared. It was Margó. Aurelia was pushing her and Rómulo Esparza followed, carrying his guitar case. Father Clark walked with them to the front of the room, the crowd suddenly fell quiet, there were whispers, and a few people applauded the entrance of the mezzo-soprano, who smiled timidly. She was wearing a simple cream-colored blouse, black slacks, and low heels. Her hair down, dark black and wavy, covering half of her face, made my heart race. There was no way she didn't see me, but she avoided looking at me. The priest wasn't sure if he should position her on the stage already or mix her in with the wheelchair gang. They decided on the stage, the priest himself pushed her there, and Margó, when she passed in front of me, ignored me once again. The one who didn't ignore me was Aurelia, who was there to escort her employer, and as soon as she recognized me, she gave me one of her lavish smiles, which everyone noticed and, consequently, made people notice me, who'd gone unnoticed until then. Some must have asked themselves what I was doing next to the bookcase, standing there doing nothing. They didn't know that I was securing part of the staging. Aurelia's unbridled smile in front of a room full of people once again made me question her sanity, and I thought that if the poor woman was nuts, Margó knew, and if she knew, she shouldn't have placed any merit on what she told her about me kissing her daughter under the table. She was too intelligent to be rattled by something so trivial. Instead, knowing that I could still hide under a table with a little girl and hold her in my arms, had made her feel hopelessly old and too inadequate for me. Perhaps she felt like I was still too restless, and that had depressed her, making her ask herself what she could offer me from her wheelchair. Her flowing hair, and her marvelous, insensitive thighs? Little Griselda had toppled her with a simple prank. I looked at her, longing for her to look back at me, but she didn't. Had she turned to look at me, she would have understood that I'd never betray her, and that her skin, her hair, and her sensuously raspy voice were so much more redeeming than her condition. Hoping for some sign from her, I'd moved away from the bookcase without realizing and I stood there, separated from it, which triggered the beginning of the disaster.

The poetry reciters, the declaimers rather, entered, all of them men and wearing tuxedos, led by the dolled-

up and glistening Amalia Reséndiz, who was wearing
an unfortunate embroidered white blouse, a huipil,
which fell to her heels. Like a murder of crows behind
a chicken, they were received by another murmur from
the audience. There were five of them and they took
their seats in the first row, which had been reserved for
them, beside Rómulo Esparza; Amalia Reséndiz sat in
the middle. I recognized three of the starchy gentlemen
who'd read at her house the week before. There were still
two empty seats, and Amalia motioned to Father Clark,
who signaled to the back of the room. Tatis Reséndiz,
wearing a spectacular olive-green evening gown and
open-toe high heels, entered on the arm of her uncle.
Humberto Reséndiz wore a tuxedo like the declaimers.
They slowed their pace so everyone could admire them;
an aura of delicate ridiculousness encircled them as
they walked toward their seats, with Tatis escorted on
her uncle's arm as if uncle and niece had mistaken the
modest bookstore stage for a church altar and the poetry
soiree for her wedding. Amalia Reséndiz, perhaps noting
how laughable the situation was, began to applaud,
followed by the declaimers, and the applause propagated
throughout the room, while Tatis and her uncle sat down
in the two remaining unoccupied seats in the first row.

Then Father Clark approached the microphone and
opened the poetic and musical soiree in honor of Isabel
Fraire, not a single book of whose could be found in the
entire bookstore.

———

IT WAS MARGÓ'S BEAUTY that convinced Amalia Reséndiz to change the program order on the spot. She'd envisioned a first part dedicated to the five orators, to be followed by Margó's musical intermezzo, and then Tatis would close the evening triumphantly. But Amalia Reséndiz must have sensed, observing Margó concentrating in her wheelchair, that she was the real gem of the evening, and she changed the order to spare her niece an unpleasant close, sending her into the fray after the last orator had returned to his seat. Not one of them had learned a single poem by Isabel Fraire, something I appreciated because they would have destroyed them, and because of the way things turned out, Isabel Fraire was mentioned only once during that tragic soiree.

Tatis Reséndiz had just situated herself in the middle of the stage when I noticed something pressing against my back, as if someone were pushing me, and it wasn't until that moment that I realized I'd moved away from the bookcase. The anchors couldn't hold the weight on the shelves, causing the bookcase to come away from the wall and a whole row of books on the top shelf fell to the floor. Tatis screamed in surprise and the towering piece of furniture, even though I tried to hold it with my back, fell over. Everyone shouted and stood up from their chairs. That's when the first shot was heard.

The bookcase hurled me onto the row of wheelchairs, which I rammed head-on, knocking three old people over with me. Then the second and third shots were heard. It was most likely the bookcase crashing down, with the subsequent scene of panic that it produced, that caused the shooter to continue firing in such a hurried manner, and that saved Tatis Reséndiz's life, wounded as she was in only one arm. The bookcase collapsed onto the stage and grazed Margó by a hair. The photograph that portrayed my landing on the wheelchairs, which coincided with the first and second gunshots, appeared the next day on the front pages of the local newspapers and led to the conclusion that I'd thrown myself on the old-timers to protect them from the gunfire, thus saving their lives. Proof that the assassin was also firing at them came from the third shot, aimed at my father who was at the far end of the row of wheelchairs. It was in fact the only shot of the three fired that found its target. The bullet entered his right temple. Margó remained motionless while the crowd screamed and rushed to the exit, her hair covered her face which, inclined over her chest, seemed to have achieved its highest degree of concentration, then blood soaked her blouse and it was ascertained that the second shot, also aimed at Tatis, was the one "that caused the death of the beautiful mezzo-soprano, who found herself right behind Señorita Reséndiz, the principle target of last night's cowardly

attack," as stated the following day in the largest
newspaper in circulation in our city.

No one could give a satisfactory explanation for the
third shot fired that evening. Most people attributed it
to the failings of an inexperienced assassin who killed
two innocent people and only wounded the arm of the
principle target, and others thought it was an act of
vandalism pure and simple. I immediately ruled out
Abigael Martínez, whose Beretta, as the investigation
revealed, wasn't loaded, and I also doubted that he
suspected that the old man reduced to skin and bones
at the far end of the row of wheelchairs was my father,
but I was never convinced by the lost-bullet theory the
press espoused.

When Güero died in a standoff with the police along
the US border one month later, I went to see Guiomar,
his wife, to pay my respects. I wasn't sure if I'd find her.
In fact, she was moving. There were boxes on the floor in
the living room and dining room, and the only furniture
remaining was a small table and two chairs where we
sat to drink the coffee she offered me. Papá called her *la
niña*, the little girl, but I never knew why. I asked where
she was moving to and she said to her parents' house, in
Sinaloa, so Irasema, her daughter, wouldn't miss out on
any of the school year. I nodded and sipped my coffee.

"Why'd you come, Eduardo?" she asked. "Just to pay your respects?"

I took another sip, burning my tongue a little.

"No, I want to ask you something."

She invited me to speak with a movement of her hand. She used her gestures sparingly, and I always thought that if she'd been ten or fifteen years older she would have been Papá's perfect match; they were made for each other, and when they were having a conversation they always lowered their voices and laughed a lot, as if they were making fun of everyone else and judging them from some Olympus exclusively their own. I told her that Güero and I had met one afternoon at Sanborns de Piedra where I'd arranged to see him to ask a favor, and I asked if he'd mentioned anything to her about our meeting.

"No."

"He didn't even tell you that we saw each other?"

"No."

"Are you sure?"

"I'd remember," she told me.

I nodded. So Güero hadn't taken me seriously. He must've thought that what I said that afternoon about my father was some knee-jerk reaction, something I'd later regret, and that's why he hadn't taken the time to tell his wife about it. Even I, who'd set up the meeting to ask him to scare the shit out of Colonel Atarriaga, couldn't remember how we'd arrived at the point in our conversation in which I asked him if he'd be capable of helping me put an end to Papá's opprobrious state. Or maybe he had taken me seriously, so seriously that he hadn't mentioned a single word of our conversation to his wife.

"What was it you wanted him to do for you?" Guiomar asked me.

"I can't tell you. I only wanted to know if he'd mentioned anything to you."

She looked outside, toward the tiny yard in front of the house, and then looked at me again.

"Your father came to see me about a year ago," she told me, "after he suffered that bout of pain in his spine."

"What pain in his spine?" I asked her.

"Your father made Celeste promise not to tell you anything."

"Why?"

"I think he was afraid you'd decide to have him hospitalized. You weren't around when it happened. It was serious, it seems, and he got scared and came to see me."

"With Celeste?"

"No, by himself in a taxi."

"Why'd he come here?"

"That I can tell you. He asked me to speak with José."

"With José?"

"My husband."

It was the first time I'd heard Güero's real name, or maybe I'd heard it at some point and after that I'd forgotten it.

"He wanted him to take care of…" she continued, but then stopped, as if she couldn't find the suitable words. She sipped her coffee and she ran a finger over the corner of her mouth. "He wanted José to make sure he didn't have to go through hell."

"Because of his cancer?"

"Yes. According to your father, in these violent times, it was the safest and most expeditious way to go. He didn't want to implicate either of you in any way, and he knew he wouldn't have the nerve to stick a pistol barrel in his mouth."

Papá'd beat me to it, I thought, and I remembered the cat in the vacant lot from my childhood, when Ofelia lifted that rock to put an end to the animal's suffering. I've never forgotten the crunch of its skull when the rock crushed it.

Guiomar took a sip of coffee and I heard the sound of the liquid going down her throat. The house, empty of its furnishings, was perfectly silent.

"Why'd he come to talk to you and not with Güero directly?" I asked her.

"Your father and José were no longer on speaking terms, you know why. Also, even though he didn't tell me, he wanted to know what I thought."

"What you thought?"

"Yes."

I stared at her. "And what did you think?"

"I told him he was crazy to ask him to do something like that."

"So you didn't tell Güero anything." I corrected myself: "Tell José."

"No."

"Are you sure?"

"Not a word."

I didn't feel like smiling, and I said, "Then how'd you figure out that was the same thing I asked Güero to do at Sanborns de Piedra?" This time I didn't correct myself and she frowned.

"I didn't know that's what you'd asked him to do."

I finished my coffee. It was really good, and I remembered that Papá always praised Guiomar's coffee.

"The truth is that I didn't actually ask him to do it, what you'd call asking. Do you have a napkin?"

She got up, went to the kitchen, and came back with a napkin holder, apologizing. She saw my empty cup and asked if I wanted more coffee.

"No, thanks. Where was I?"

"You didn't ask him to do it, actually." She sat down again.

"I set up a meeting to ask him for a favor and he told me he couldn't do it. Then, during the conversation, the thing about my father came up. I didn't ask him to do anything, I only wanted to know if I could count on him, if it were necessary."

"Of course, because of everything he owed you and your father." I noticed the bitterness in her voice and looked away, observing the cardboard boxes piled in a corner of the room. "And what did he tell you?" she asked looking straight into my eyes.

I raised the cup to my mouth, knowing it was empty, and she, seeing me do it, didn't ask if I wanted more coffee.

"That I should mind my own business," I answered. "That I should leave it up to my father. I thought they'd come to an agreement. And now you tell me my father came to see you to ask Güero to—"

"José never knew your father came to see me!" she interrupted. "I already told you that. And I doubt your father spoke with him afterward."

"Why?"

"I already told you they weren't on speaking terms," she answered at once, lowering her voice. "Your father was really frightened about his spine and he wanted to know if he could cut his losses when the time came, that's why he came to see me, and he called beforehand to make sure they wouldn't run into each other."

"So he left here knowing you weren't going to—"

"I told him I'd think about it. I know how impulsive your father was. A moment of impulse brought him here, and I thought it would pass."

"And couldn't it be that José listened to me when I asked him to do the same thing at Sanborns de Piedra?"

"No, he wouldn't have listened to you, only your father."

The house fell back into that oppressive silence that precedes a move and I could hear Guiomar's breathing. I didn't know if I should believe her. If she was lying, if she'd conveyed the message to Güero, and he'd acted accordingly, paying off in one fell swoop all the debt he owed us, I'd never find out, now that he was dead.

I looked at the pile of cardboard boxes again and asked if she needed help.

"Thanks, it's okay." She got up and took the two cups to the kitchen. I also got up and went to the window that looked onto the little yard. It was starting to get dark outside.

When she came back to the living room, I told her, "Don't mention a word of this to Ofelia, it would give her a heart attack if she knew why my father came to see you."

"Your sister knows."

I turned around. "What'd you say?"

She was standing next to the table.

"Your father told her. When he spoke with me, he'd already talked to your sister, he needed her approval and she gave it to him."

I must have made a face of complete disbelief, because Guiomar softened her voice so she wouldn't hurt my feelings.

"They didn't want to tell you anything, Eduardo, because you live in your own little world."

I noticed the plural, which included my father.

"My father told you that? That I'm living in my own little world?"

"More or less."

She took the napkin holder back to the kitchen. I had a feeling she did it to give me time to recover from the effect her words had on me. Even though my sister had only been around to hear a fraction of his agony from the pain in his bones and his shrieking when he couldn't move his bowels, my father had confided in her instead of me. Ofelia had hidden that she was prepared to aid and abet my father in his desire to decide at what moment, with Güero's help, he was going to cut his losses, to use Guiomar's terminology, and then it all made sense. She was also aware of the protection fee. If not, how else would my father have explained that Güero owed him a debt and was willing to pay it any way he could? My sister was aware of the fee and of, most likely, Papá's bout of spinal pain. I came close to asking Guiomar about it, but I decided to spare her the discomfort I was going to put her in, because it was clear that the only person no one told anything to was me, the kid who lived in his own little world, or in his bubble, as Margó had said.

I went out to the yard while I waited for Guiomar to come back from the kitchen, and I looked at the trees along the street, submerging myself in their majestic foliage. Maybe that was my problem, not looking at what was directly in front of me but sinking into it instead, whether with objects or people. In doing so, I betrayed the nature of what put itself in front of me. In me, perceptiveness was not a virtue but a form of evasion. I used to lose sight of the simple and plain prose of the world. Maybe only when I was waiting for an hour outside the bank to take a picture of Rosario that I knew would make my father happy was I truly part of it.

Either way, the death of my father threw me into a series of hasty acts of which I was an extremely efficient executor, although passive, or efficient because I was passive, as if the bookcase that fell and triggered the tragedy continued pushing me from behind with its enormous weight, which was perhaps my only way to feel reality's heartbeat or, in other words, of not losing sight of the skin of everything, the skin that is so close at hand and so elusive, so explicit and unobtainable, like Margó's, which I was never able to touch.

Thanks to my alleged heroic act that night in El Caracol, the parole board pardoned me from the community service hours I still had to complete, and they even returned my driver's license, which I burned as soon as I had it in my hands. We put Papá's house up for sale and settled up with Celeste, who'd been with us for close to four years, and when I asked her if she wanted me to write a letter of recommendation for some future employment, she assured me that it wasn't necessary and I didn't need to ask her where she was going to live from then on. I saw Aurelia for the last time at Margó's wake, which was attended by a multitude. Everyone wanted to pay their last respects to the most famous mezzo-soprano in the City of Eternal Spring, despite the fact that no one, except Rómulo Esparza, had heard her sing. Her world debut was cut short by bad luck and her voice would forever remain shrouded in mystery. Aurelia looked unhinged. Someone had made her understand that her employer was gone forever. When I hugged her, her ear-to-ear grin rematerialized but it disappeared again when we parted. Two days later I went back to the house to ask her for the picture of Margó wearing a bathing suit over that oblong cubist body of hers. She wasn't there. The next-door neighbor told me she'd gone back to her hometown with her daughter, without leaving any contact information. I went back a few months later, hoping to find Margó's sister and ask her for the nightstand photograph, and the same neighbor informed me that the house had been sold. I don't have any other picture of Margó than the two or three faded ones that came out in the paper after her death, and in those I have a hard time recognizing the woman whose skin I fell in love with, and from whom the only thing I received was a kiss on the cheek.

Father Clark left the home reading program, which remained entirely under the city council's management

from then on. We sold my father's house, and with my
share of the sale I bought a small apartment where I live
now. The Valverde Furniture Store grew in popularity,
and for the next three months we had exceptional sales,
after which I sold it and settled up with Jaime, and
I've heard nothing from him since. During that time
of abundance no one came to take over for David and
people of that ilk for their punctual monthly collections.
I suppose my public notoriety, which earned me the
nickname "Hero of the Golden-Agers," was enough
prompting for the mobsters to stay away from the
furniture store, at least for a while, and so, after I sold
it, I decided to open an orthotics shop for the elderly
and handicapped, which revealed itself to be a lucrative
business, because our city, due to the unchecked danger
it suffers from, is expelling young people and keeping
only the old-timers around, like any other godforsaken
town of emigrants. The restaurants, except Sanborns,
are going extinct; half of the mansions are up for sale;
the bougainvillea on the fences are rotting; and I guess
pretty soon we'll hold the world record for the city with
the most empty swimming pools.

Abigael Martínez closed El Caracol and opened a
new bookstore in Querétaro. Obviously he didn't want
to take the bookcases that had belonged to my father
with him and he called me three months later to tell me
that he'd found a copy of Isabel Fraire's collected poems
and that he'd like to exchange it for my copy, so he could

keep the one Isabel had inscribed for him. We sent our respective copies through the mail and that was our last contact.

Even though I was released from the home reading program, I haven't stopped going to the Vigils' house. Of all my former hosts, theirs is the only house I continue to visit. Thanks to Gianni Rodari, of whom we've read all the poems we could find, the father was convinced that his children are not deaf. Now they go to a regular school and only live deaf lives in their house. Undeafening them, so to speak, has been the greatest achievement of my short career as a home reader. After Rodari, we read other poets, among them Isabel Fraire. The whole family learned to listen to poetry, the three children with their ears, and the father, the mother, and the grandmother by reading my lips, because even with the mere movement of my lips, poetry allows itself to be heard, something I didn't know but learned in that house. I also learned to shake off my inherent deafness in their home, to emerge a little, amid so many deaf people, from my bubble, and to know what I'm saying when I hear myself say it. And that's how I turned thirty-five. It was my birthday the other day and the Vigils invited me to their house to celebrate it with them. They turned out the lights, it was quiet, and I sat back and watched the whole family emerge from the kitchen carrying a cake with thirty-five flaming candles and start to sing "Las Mañanitas," but in the penumbra created by the candles it wasn't "The

Morning Song" that I heard but the words my father
loved and those that touched Margó so deeply, which
she couldn't sing the night of her world debut and the
Vigils sang in chorus, standing and carefully situated,
while I listened to them with an adolescent shiver, and
I was thankful for the darkness that hid me from their
gaze: "Your skin, like sheets of sand and sheets of water
swirling. Your skin, with its louring mandolin brilliance.
Your skin, where my skin arrives as if coming home
and lights a silenced lamp. Your skin, that nourishes my
eyes and wears my name like a new dress. Your skin, a
mirror where my skin recognizes me and my lost hand
comes back from my childhood and reaches this present
moment and greets me. Your skin, where at last I am
with myself."

May 2016–February 2017